THE DOOR IN THE FOREST

RODERICK TOWNLEY

Knopf
new york

THIS IS A BORZOI BOOK PUBLISHED BY ALFRED A. KNOPF

Visit us on the Web! www.randomhouse.com/kids

Educators and librarians, for a variety of teaching tools, visit us at www.randomhouse.com/teachers

Library of Congress Cataloging-in-Publication Data
Townley, Rod.
The door in the forest / Roderick Townley. — 1st ed.
p. cm.
"A Borzoi book."
Summary: While trying to outwit the soldiers who are occupying their small town, fourteen-year-old Daniel, who cannot lie, and Emily, who discovers she has magical powers, are inexplicably drawn to a mysterious island in the heart of the forest where townsfolk have been warned never to go.
ISBN 978-0-375-85601-3 (trade) — ISBN 978-0-375-95601-0 (lib. bdg.) —
ISBN 978-0-375-89700-9 (ebook)
[1. Honesty—Fiction. 2. Magic—Fiction. 3. Soldiers—Fiction. 4. Space and time—Fiction.] I. Title.
PZ7.T64965Doo 2011
[Fic]—dc22
2010034710

The text of this book is set in 12-point Goudy.
Printed in the United States of America
March 2011
10 9 8 7 6 5 4 3 2 1
First Edition

For Wyatt—
to say the least

Part One
THERE

CONTENTS

Part Two
HERE

Part Three
NOW

Lady, three white leopards sat under a juniper tree.
—T. S. Eliot

Part One
THERE

S One
trangers

Some people claimed it was enchanted; others swore it was cursed; but, really, it hardly mattered what you thought because you couldn't get to it. The place pushed back against all your attempts, setting out twisted thickets of hedge-apple trees bristling with curved, medieval-looking thorns. After that came ankle-catching thistles, firethorn, baneberry, and poison oak. If at last you reached the creek, you'd peer across at an impervious curtain of leaves that never crisped or fell with the change of seasons, and vines that stitched the island shut like a coat.

From most sides, it wasn't even visible, a patch of wildness encircled by water and wedged in a tangle of undergrowth.

There was one place you could almost see the island as an island, and that was where Daniel was today, at his favorite watching place on the footbridge over a contributing brook, a half mile from his house. On breezy afternoons, the foliage might swing briefly aside to let him see the green darken almost to night before his sunstruck eyes.

He pushed away a flop of dirty-blond hair and looked down at the line of ripples where the clear water of the tributary met the sullen brown of the stream around the island. Three streams, really, cloudy and bedded in quicksand. That was another barrier, the quicksand. Just ask Widow Beinemann, whose dog jumped in after a stick two summers ago and was sucked down before he could whimper.

Daniel was fascinated by the stories, by the impenetrable green wall before him, and more than anything by the poisonous, white-headed water snakes that wound their lazy S's through the current. The legend was that the snakes had human faces, though he hadn't gotten close enough to be sure.

The boy leaned against the railing and felt the wind finger his hair. He had not given up hope of finding a way across. There wasn't much adventure to be had in the farming town of Everwood; but here was an adventure that had been staring him in the face all his life, and all he could do was stare back.

Imagine exploring this forbidden place where no one had ever been—never, since the moist beginnings of life on earth. It was in this one way like the moon, a land where no one had ever died and no one had ever been born. A place where no one had ever told a lie.

That was important to Daniel, because he too had never lied. It wasn't that he was especially virtuous. He just couldn't. He got blinding headaches when he tried. If he tried *really* hard, he'd get a stomach ache as well. Once, he'd almost thrown up. The doctor didn't believe him. And anyway, wasn't telling the truth a virtue?

It wasn't such a virtue in school, where the other kids called him "the snitch." That's when they weren't making fun of his tall, skinny frame and unruly hair. Girls were especially hard on him. They were full of secrets they didn't want told. They considered Daniel dangerous, and not in a good way. There was a reason he spent most of his time by himself.

Suddenly he realized there was someone—no, not a person, a heron, tall as a man—standing across the creek, and his heart thumped guiltily, as if he'd been caught by a teacher. Had it been there the whole time, or magically materialized? A great blue heron it was, imperious with its dark cap and accusing eyes. A brush of white feathers flowed back over its cheek like a trail of smoke. Daniel had seen the bird before, always on the other side, immobile on its stick legs, and it gave him a strange feeling, as if there were a special message meant for him alone, if only he could figure it out.

"Fly me across!" he called.

The bird's pipe-cleaner neck lowered into a tight S and its yellow eyes glared.

"Yes, you!" Daniel yelled. "You can do it."

"Who ya yelling at?" came a voice behind him.

Daniel whirled around, blushing. It was only Wes, his kid brother.

"Take a look."

Wesley rested his chin on the railing. "Oooh."

Being ten, he immediately bent down, picked up a stone, and threw it.

"Stop it!" Daniel snapped.

"I want to see him fly."

"Leave him alone!"

Wesley's mouth tightened. "You're always bossing me around."

"Sometimes you need bossing."

"I'm as smart as you."

Daniel eased into a smile. "No, Wes, you're smarter. But sometimes you do dumb things."

Wesley frowned at his shoes. With his sharp, serious features, ironed shirt, and khaki shorts, he looked like a tiny accountant. Actually, he was dressed for summer school. Completely voluntary on his part—he just wanted to learn more about geography, his favorite subject. Daniel had sometimes caught him studying maps long after bedtime. Ten years from now, he could be wearing a suit and living in the city. He might even sail off to those foreign countries he was always reading about. Daniel would still be here kicking around in blue jeans.

Probably he'd still be looking for a way onto the island.

"Come on," said Daniel. "Let's go see Dad. We can grab something to eat."

Wesley glanced at the heron. He had another stone, aching to be thrown, which he turned around in his fingers. He let it drop.

They reached the road, a strip of hard-packed dirt between fields. A tractor puttered by, old Wayne Eccles looking down from his rickety throne. "Hey, boys," he called. The brothers gave a wave and watched as the contraption continued down the road. They always watched when something with a motor came by, it was so rare. Good old Eccles.

Wes kicked pebbles ahead of him as he walked, but had

to abandon that to keep up with his brother's strides. Sometimes it seemed he was always hurrying to catch up and never could. Couldn't throw a ball as hard, couldn't run as fast. It was the curse of being four years younger.

Suddenly Daniel stopped, squinting ahead at distant forms wavering in the afternoon heat. *Strangers,* he realized. As they came closer, he amended that: *strangers from the city.* Finally, seeing them clearly: *a family.*

Daniel raised a hand, but the little group passed without a word or sign, the father pulling a cart creaking with sad-looking possessions, the woman, blank-eyed, holding an infant against her shoulder, while a boy of six or seven walked beside them. He stared at Daniel and Wes as if they'd done something bad to him personally.

The boys stared back. People you saw on the road always gave you a hello at least. But the moment passed, and the family went on, the creaking of the cart diminishing.

"Who were *they?*" said Wesley.

"Refugees from the city. I saw some yesterday, too."

"You mean"—the boy hesitated—"it's starting?"

"Looks that way."

Daniel picked up the pace and his brother hustled to keep up. "I thought it was over," Wes said.

"The Uncertainties? They're never over for long."

The boys continued on. Soon they came to houses that had yards instead of fields. There was the post office ahead, a building so tiny and tight you'd think it'd been built by the third little pig. After that came the hardware store, the columned municipal building, the old schoolhouse, and then Crowley's, the town's one grocery, owned by the boys' father.

Daniel stumped up the steps while his brother took the ramp at a run. Inside it wasn't much cooler than out, although a wobbly ceiling fan groaned overhead, circulating the smells of coffee beans and cheddar. Crowley's was a friendly place and the boys liked coming, even if it meant helping out. They especially liked the fact that the store had electricity. Most of the buildings in town were electrified and had been for years; but the lines hadn't yet been run out to the farms. It felt good standing in front of the refrigeration case, as Daniel did now, cooling himself. No need for ice blocks here.

Wesley was writing his initials in the sawdust with the toe of his sneaker. "Who's Dad talking to?"

John Crowley was behind the counter, shaking his head and smiling at an elderly man and his tiny wife, her iron curls held in a kerchief. She was counting out coins.

"No, no, you keep your money," Crowley said, bending over them. Angular and perpetually tipped forward, he bent over all his customers.

"We pay what we owe," she replied, giving him a hard look.

Two potatoes and a box of crackers lay on the counter. The woman's husband raised a trembly hand. His flyaway hair wavered under the ceiling fan.

Crowley understood about pride. "At least take a bottle of water," he said.

They started to object, but he was ahead of them. "It's an advertising special. Today only. Every customer gets a bottle of water."

It's hard to argue with an advertising special. The couple

mumbled something, slid the water and groceries into a bag, and wobbled away. Crowley watched through the window. As they reached the street, the sun obliterated them like an overexposed photograph.

"You know them, Dad?" said Daniel.

His father shook his head. "From the city."

Wesley looked up from the display rack of candy bars. "Can I have one?"

"One."

"We're not in danger," said Daniel, "are we?"

"I don't think so. There's nothing in this town anybody wants. It's the advantage of not having anything."

"Then I hope we never get anything."

"Also . . ." Crowley waggled his hand.

"I know," said Daniel. "We're protected."

"That's what they say."

A breeze on the back of his neck made Daniel turn as Melinda Olsen and her mother came into the store. His stomach dropped, as it usually did when Mel appeared. She caught sight of him, and he thought he saw her eyes flicker. She adjusted her tapestry-covered shoulder bag. "Hi, Danny." Bright and casual, with not a trace of warmth.

"Hi, Mel. Hi, Mrs. Olsen."

"Hello, Daniel," said the mother. She nodded to his dad. "Mr. Crowley."

They went past the vegetable bins, Melinda's white sundress swerving behind her.

Crowley smiled at his son. "Did I lose you, Danny?"

"No, it's just . . ."

"Just a very pretty girl. Yes, I can see."

Wesley gave a disgusted look. "Just a mean girl."

Daniel shushed him. "You don't know what you're talking about." Really, he didn't blame Melinda for not liking him. It wasn't just that he was too skinny and too tall, although he was sure that figured in. It was that, when quizzed directly by the biology teacher, he had admitted to letting Mel copy his answers on an in-class quiz. How he wished he could have lied at that moment! There is no greater crime than telling on another kid.

"What were we talking about?" said Crowley.

Daniel remembered. "Do you think it's true that we're protected?"

"Who knows? People around here are superstitious. They don't think they are, but they are. You ask a farmer why he plants an old sock in the corner of his field, he'll look at you like you're crazy. He'll say, 'I'd be a damn fool if I didn't!' "

"I heard that."

"Like it's just common sense."

Daniel shook his head.

"Still," said Crowley, leaning back against the register. "All my life there've been the Uncertainties. They've never touched us in Everwood." Rubbing his chin, "Of course, there's always a first time." He watched Wesley pocket a second candy bar. "Say, you boys planning to help me or not?"

The next morning, after his chores, Daniel hurried out of the house, jumping down the two stone slabs to the yard. The day was already hot, but it was better than being inside.

Reaching the road, he ran into his next-door neighbor, a big tattooed man named Fish, who despite his name raised chickens. "You notice we been getting a lot of strangers lately?" Fish said. He folded his bare arms, covering the coiled snake on his biceps.

"Yesterday," the boy answered quickly, anxious to get on, "we passed some on the road."

"Well," said Fish, nodding, "looks like we got some more."

Far up the road, a dark spot rippled in the heat waves. As they watched, the spot grew larger and separated into two spots, one taller than the other.

"Do you know them?" said Daniel.

"Hard to say."

The larger spot elongated into a man. As he came closer, they could see he was not much over thirty, but he didn't move young. His hat was dented in the wrong places, and his suitcase pulled him sideways, putting him off his stride. Beside him walked a girl, Daniel's age or a little less, swinging a cloth bag bulging with belongings. Dirty to begin with, she scuffled up clouds of dust with her sandals.

Fish called up to his wife, Min, but it was John Crowley who came out. He still had a few minutes before he had to leave for the store.

"Take a look," said Fish. "Isn't that Stecher?"

Crowley ducked back in to grab a couple of apples from the bin behind the door and a jar of water from the sink. He stood holding them as the strange pair approached.

"Morning, Arthur," he said. "Long time."

The man put down the suitcase and touched his hat

brim. He cast his eye around. "I see nothing's changed in Never Good." His voice was thin and had a catch to it.

"Yes, Everwood is always the same," said Crowley, "and we like it well enough."

The man's pale lashes blinked. "Well, it was always Never Good to me."

"I'm thinking you and your daughter could use a drink of water," Crowley said. He threw a smile at the girl, but she didn't catch it. She was looking at her feet.

The man took the jar. Daniel watched, waiting for the thank-you, but it didn't come. "Ain't no daughter."

"Oh?" said Crowley.

The stranger tilted back the jar, took a long drink, then removed his hat and poured the rest over his head. The caked dirt turned to muddy rivulets and dripped from his chin.

Everyone stared at him, even the girl.

"Where you headed?" said Crowley.

"Old lady Byrdsong."

Crowley looked at him narrowly. "What do you want with Mrs. Byrdsong?"

The man didn't meet his eyes. Daniel realized he hadn't met anyone's eyes the whole time.

"I said what do you want with her?"

The man nodded toward the girl. "I'm to leave this one with her."

"And why is that?"

"It's her grandma."

Daniel glanced from his dad to the miserable-looking girl. The thing she was dressed in might once have been nice, before it was torn under one arm, soaked by rain, and coated in dust. Was she really Bridey Byrdsong's granddaughter? Everybody knew Bridey was dotty. Also, she was a witch. A good one, probably, but still.

By now, other neighbors had come out onto the road, among them Daniel's mother, Gwen. She went right over and knelt beside the girl. "What's your name, dear?"

The girl looked at her silently.

"She don't talk much," said the man. "Fact, she don't talk at all."

Mrs. Crowley took an apple and put it in the child's hand. The girl stared at it as if she'd never seen such a thing before.

"Take it. It's for you."

The girl looked up at the man for permission. He shrugged. Still, she didn't eat it. Daniel wondered briefly if she knew how.

"You say you're not her father?" said Gwen, standing up and brushing her apron.

"Uncle."

"Uncle! You mean this is . . . ?"

"Miranda's kid, yeah."

Gwen looked at her closely. The girl was so dirty it was hard to tell what she looked like under it all. Even her eyes, a noncommittal brown, were hard to get a sense of.

"Why's she with you?" You could see Gwen Crowley was about fed up with Arthur Stecher. "Where is her mother?"

"Likely dead."

Mrs. Crowley instinctively reached for the girl's shoulder. "What makes you say that?"

"Always sticking her neck out. Talking to people you don't talk to. I wasn't surprised."

"Surprised at *what?*"

"Soldiers came and took her."

Everyone was quiet. The girl looked down.

"We had to get out quick, Emily and me."

"Emily. Now I remember," said Mrs. Crowley.

"She's a strange one."

"Strange how?"

He shrugged. "Don't talk. Ornery. I can't take care of her. Can't hardly take care of myself."

"I can believe that." Mrs. Crowley's voice was flat. She'd seen the business with the water jar. "We'll see she gets to Bridey."

Stecher nodded. "Better I don't see the old bat. I didn't leave on such a good note."

"I remember." Mr. Crowley nodded.

Daniel looked at Stecher, trying to figure him out. The man might tell the truth, but he had liar's eyes and a mouth made for excuses.

"Well," the man said, "I'll be pushing on, then." He took off his hat, punched it from the inside, and stuck it back on his head. "Spare a little money for the road?"

"Sorry," said Crowley. "You can have an apple, though."

Stecher hesitated, blinking, then took the apple and rubbed it on his shirt. Without a word or a glance at the girl, he hoisted the suitcase, steadied himself, and started off.

"Mad creature," Mrs. Crowley said under her breath. She might have said more, but not with the girl there. "Come on, Emily," she said. "Let's go inside and get some real food in you."

Mr. Crowley rubbed his chin. "Somebody," he said, "needs to run over and tell Bridey. Danny, will you do that?"

"I guess."

"I'd go, but I need to get to the store."

"Quick as you can now, Danny," said his mother, heading inside. "I can use your help."

Why did they always have to ask him? "Okay," he said.

She nodded. "Run along, then."

"I'm *going*." So much for his free time. He watched glumly as Mr. Fish and the other neighbors stood around and kicked the dirt, paying him no attention. They quietly cursed the government. Then, for good measure, they cursed the refugees who'd brought their problems on themselves.

"Now they'll be expecting us to take care of them," said Fish.

Daniel thought that was unfair. The last time the Uncertainties had come, there'd been beggars, sure, but they'd always been polite and hadn't stayed long. Could they help being hungry? Or having the wrong politics?

He watched as the men drifted away, then he started down the road toward Grandma Byrdsong's. The day's heat was building. The leaves on the overhanging elms were dusty and motionless, holding their breath.

That's when he saw the shadow flit across the road. He looked up in time to see a great blue heron sail silently overhead.

The Call

Grandma Byrdsong was taking a bath. More exactly, she was watching the bubbles in her bath as, one by one, they silently burst, causing continents of suds to re-form in new patterns. Since she was a considerable person, and not the most nimble, she'd raised great quantities of suds when she'd first walrussed into the tub. Once settled, she remained submerged to her thick neck, watching.

Some people tell fortunes by reading tea leaves. That had never worked for Bridey Byrdsong. It was suds. Suds were the way to see what was what, and what was going to be what in this world.

Besides, it made her arthritis feel better.

Today was unusual. She wasn't in the habit of taking baths in the middle of the day, or even every day, since the old house was not blessed with running water—just several large barrels, strategically placed in kitchen and bath, that had to be filled periodically from the pump. But today, as she'd gazed into the vanity mirror to darken her eyebrows and pink her cheeks, her reflection had spoken to her. She never knew when it would, or what it would say. This time it said, "Bridey Byrdsong, you put down that eyebrow pencil, heat up the water, and climb into the bath."

No whys or wherefores. Just "climb into the bath." So that is what she did, and that was where Daniel found her when he arrived.

"Hold on there, Danny," she called through the bathroom door. Actually, through two doors with a hallway between. She had a big voice when it was needed.

"No hurry," he called back. He didn't mind having a few minutes to look around. He loved the old place, and the old lady who enlivened it, and he didn't see why everybody thought she was so strange. Odd, yes. For one thing, she'd kept her own name, although she'd been married. All the Byrdsong women did, apparently. Once a Byrdsong, always a Byrdsong. Daniel remembered Mrs. Fish shaking her head about it. But what was so awful about keeping your own name? These were modern times.

He went into the sitting room, where there was a painting he especially liked. It showed a clearing with wind-bent grasses tipped with sunlight. In the middle stood a swaying oak tree, and beneath it a blanket, a picnic basket, and a bottle of wine. The only thing missing was people. The painting was titled simply *Here*.

Daniel was also taken with a mirror by the front door that showed not your face, but the back of your head. It was to help you fix your hair, or adjust your hat, Bridey had once explained, before you went out. Daniel stood before it now, examining a blond cowlick that his comb had never managed to tame.

At the same moment, Mrs. Byrdsong was examining a dwindling peninsula of suds in the cooling tub. There was something she didn't understand, and it bothered her. She cast her eye over the bubbles and the pattern of their bursting. The message was clear, but the meaning obscure. She was supposed to pass the necklace on. And not to the person she thought. Curious.

With a sigh, she reached for the towel and hoisted herself up. She'd seen what there was to see.

"You'll find a plate of cookies on the counter," she yelled out. "Fresh this morning."

"I see them. Thanks."

"Leave a few for the rest of us."

Ten minutes later, she emerged, heavily scented and bangled, like a ship from the East under full sail. Two of her numerous cats trotted ahead of her.

"My," she said, "you're getting to be a tall drink of water."

That was what she always said, and Daniel, who was self-conscious about his height, never knew what to answer. He was supposed to come up with something, he knew. "You're all dressed up," he said, finally.

"We're having a visitor. I don't want to make a bad impression."

"How'd you know? Do you know who she is?"

"She?" Bridey tried the word on in her mind. "No. The suds only tell me so much."

"The man said she's your granddaughter."

"Ah." She broke a cookie and slowly ate the bigger half. "Emily," she said.

"That's it. We have her over at the house."

She put her hand briefly over her mouth, to hold in the crumbs. "And Miranda?"

"Who?"

"Emily's mother."

"They said she was arrested."

"Arrested!" A crumb caught in her throat and sent her into a spasm of coughing that ended only when Daniel pounded her on the back.

She nodded and waved him away, her eyes watering.

Miranda—arrested? The suds had said nothing about that. She sipped from the glass of water Daniel brought her. Miranda might have changed in the six years since she'd moved away, but she had not been, growing up, the sort who would last long in a government prison. Not *this* government.

"Danny," she said, her voice a little wobbly, "would you help me upstairs? There's something I need."

"Tell me where it is. I'll get it." He remembered the last time he'd helped her get up the stairs, only to have her forget what she'd come for.

"It needs me to find it," she said, reaching for her cane.

The help that Daniel gave was to walk behind her as she toiled through semidarkness up a narrowing staircase that every eight steps made a left-angled turn. Then it was every six steps, then every four, the house sharpening to a turret. Daniel's function, he realized with some alarm, was to catch Grandma Byrdsong in case she lost her grip on the banister and fell backward.

"Here we are!" she gasped, reaching the landing. "The Four Seasons room."

"The what?"

"It was Miranda's. She loved that music. *The Four Seasons?* She used to play it on the Victrola all the time. So I made her a special bedroom."

"I see."

He didn't see, of course, nor did he notice anything special when they went in. It was just a small, stuffy room under the eaves. Grandma Byrdsong asked him to let in a little air while she rummaged through the bureau. He went to one of the four windows and stood, trying to figure it out. It was the kind that opened outward, like spreading wings, when you turned a crank. But this window had two handles. He shrugged and turned the one on the left. As soon as the panes parted, he cried out to see snowflakes dash in, chased by a freezing wind.

"Not that one! Not that one!" shouted Bridey.

He quickly cranked the window shut.

"That's the winter window. I should have warned you."

"The winter . . ."

"Try the autumn one. Over there."

Daniel crossed the room and stood uncertainly. Everything looked normal outside—hot high summer. The handyman was by the side of the house hoeing the vegetable garden. He was shirtless and his back gleamed with sweat.

"Come on, Danny," said Bridey, pulling out a groaning bureau drawer. "What are you waiting for? I can't breathe."

Again, two handles. He turned the one on the right. The panes parted and the handyman disappeared. Dry leaves gusted past on a fresh breeze. He stared out, amazed to see the trees divesting themselves and the whole west lawn covered in red and yellow.

"But it's barely August!"

"Not out that window it isn't. Ah," she said, "here we go!" She was examining a small oblong box she'd pulled from the second-to-bottom drawer. "Danny, really! Stop playing with the windows."

Going down proved easier than climbing up. This time he was required to walk in front of Bridey, again in case she fell. She was very afraid of falling, but not as afraid as he was that she'd fall on *him*.

Daniel felt a little dazed as they reached the parlor floor. He was still trying to understand those windows.

Grandma Byrdsong paused in front of the backwards mirror in the hall and put on her hat. "Well," she said, marshaling her forces, "shall we go?"

"Right." He held open the door, and she turned her body to get through it, then gripped his hand as they crossed the porch and descended three creaking steps to the yard. The garage, which also served as a hotel for wasps, was farther away than she liked to walk, but she didn't trust anyone, certainly not a boy, to fetch her Ford sedan and drive up to the door. Grandma Byrdsong owned one of the few cars in Everwood. It had been old and cranky when she'd bought it, and it was older and crankier now.

She wasn't in such a good mood herself. She let out little gasps as she toiled ahead, as much side to side as forward, leaning alternately on the boy and on her cane.

"Wait," she commanded as they passed the vegetable

garden, a wild profusion of colors and tendrils climbing the chicken-wire fence. "Go pick a couple of tomatoes to bring your mother."

"Sure!" He ran and opened the rickety gate just as the handyman was coming out, wiping his face with his shirt. They exchanged nods and Daniel went in. The garden was not large, but it was talked about throughout the town and beyond. Daniel could understand why, kneeling to pick an oversized tomato in exactly the shape of a Bartlett pear, and another in the shape of a zucchini. You never knew what you'd find in Bridey Byrdsong's garden. Sometimes you had to bite into one of her fantastic vegetables to be sure what it was.

"Come on, Danny. I can't stand up much longer," she called.

He rejoined her, and they went on. Ahead he could see the snub nose of her car poking out of the garage. When they reached it, Bridey was too out of breath to speak. She opened the car door and had Daniel brace her elbow as she lifted her leg onto the running board. Once there, she turned and positioned herself, then let her body fall backward onto the seat.

Her left leg didn't quite make it.

"My foot, if you don't mind, Daniel," she said.

The boy knelt, got a good grip, and hoisted her foot up and in.

She winced. "Thank you, Daniel," she said. "You're a good boy. Always were."

She turned the key in the ignition. *Cheh-cheh-cheh-cheh-cheh.* The engine rumbled, then coughed and died.

Cheh-cheh-cheh-cheh-cheh-cheh-cheh-cheh-cheh-cheh.

"How about a push?" she said. Bridey made a habit of parking the car facing out, as it often needed a push to get going.

Daniel was usually the one to do the pushing. That wasn't a problem. The car wasn't all that heavy, just a black metal box with wood spoke wheels and narrow tires. But pushing the car with Grandma Byrdsong in it *was* a problem. By the time the engine stuttered into life, he was itching with sweat. He ran alongside, hopped in, and pulled the squealing door shut.

As a driver, Bridey had a way of drifting to the right, but they made the trip without incident or accident, although they left a number of terrified chickens in their wake.

Gwen was waiting at the door. "Bridey, hello! Come in. Are these for us? Wonderful!" She took the tomatoes and led the way to the kitchen. "She won't eat," she said, keeping her voice low. "And she's not speaking. I'm not sure she can."

"Really? Last time I saw her, she was babbling nonstop."

"The last time you saw her, she was six years old!"

Bridey shook her head wonderingly. "Imagine!"

They found the girl on a stool at the kitchen table, her plate of chicken and candied sweet potatoes untouched. With her blank expression and filthy red-checked dress, she had the look of a dried-out field flower someone had carelessly stuck in a vase. The truth was, her grandmother barely recognized her. This was no six-year-old. Closer to thirteen.

"I warmed up what we had last night," said Gwen.

"I'm sure it's fine." Bridey turned to the girl. "Emily," she said, smiling. The smile deepened as she took her in. "Emily, Emily."

The girl looked at her blankly.

"I've been trying to get her to eat for an hour."

Bridey laid a hand on Gwen's shoulder. "Why don't you leave us for a bit? See what I can do."

Gwen nodded.

"And could you shut the door?"

Mrs. Crowley blushed, but did as she was told.

"What's happening, Mom?" said Wesley, bouncing downstairs with a fat library book under his arm. It was one of his favorites, called *Now You See It,* about optical illusions.

She put a finger to her lips. "Grandma Byrdsong's here."

"Oh." This was a fact of no interest to a ten-year-old. He kept going, grabbing two apples from the barrel by the door, one for himself, one for the first horse he met.

Daniel and his mother went out back to pick some mint. When they returned, the kitchen door was still closed.

Daniel went up to it and listened. "She's singing!"

"Who's singing?"

"Grandma Byrdsong. Listen."

Gwen went over, but just then the door swung open. The old woman filled it completely. "Do you happen to have any jam?" she said.

"I think so." Gwen went to open the cupboard, but then stopped, seeing the girl tearing hunks of bread with her teeth as if ripping the heart out of an enemy. Except for some chicken bones, her plate was clean.

"The jam?" Bridey prompted.

Gwen found the jar of preserves. "Have you gotten her to speak?"

"We . . . communicate," she said. "Haven't gotten around to actual words yet."

"I'm sure you will."

"I know we will." The women watched as Emily wolfed the bread and jam and then washed it down with milk. "Well," said Bridey after a while, "time we were going. Ready, Emily?"

Gwen didn't like to admit she was relieved. It was tricky enough, in these lean times, to feed her own family. "Danny, why don't you go with them and help get Emily settled?"

Daniel glanced from one woman to the other. There went his day. "Sure," he said.

Ten minutes later, with the girl in the front beside her grandmother and Daniel jouncing about in the broken-springed backseat, they were on their way, raising a tunnel of dust behind them along the dirt road. Bridey had opened the split windshield to let in air, but then closed it against dust and bugs. Emily didn't seem to notice. She stared out at pastures and windbreaks, a house, a horse, a barn all whizzing by at something like twenty miles an hour—a crazy speed!

Between the seats, Daniel observed the silent girl in the front, with her cloth bag of belongings beside her. Her smudged dress, snub nose, and impossible hair gave her the look of a vagabond; but she had one prized possession at least, something in her lap she kept fingering. A toy? No, a necklace, he now saw. It looked like a cheap string of funny-shaped pearls.

She rubbed them as she might a rosary, for luck and comfort. She could use a lot of both, he thought. Bouncing along, he found himself grateful for the racket the car was making—a "bucket of bolts," the old lady had called it. It made the girl's silence less awkward. Less *audible*, in a way. How long had she been like this? Daniel didn't really remember her from when she'd lived here before.

And how was it she hadn't come to see her grandmother in all those years? The city was fifty miles away, far enough, but not one visit in six years?

His reverie was interrupted by a startling sight. Up ahead, taking up most of the road, marched a company of soldiers led by a muddy staff car, several old Crossley military vehicles, and two armored trucks. Taking up the rear was a slow-moving, house-sized monster topped by a cannon barrel that protruded like a horn. The tank shimmered in its own heat waves while its great heart roared and metal treads clanked down the road. Daniel knew such things had been used in the Great War, which had ended back in 1918, five long years ago. Perhaps this weapon had been taken out of retirement and adapted for the little wars—the Uncertainties—that plagued his own land. But why would a tank be coming to Everwood, a nothing little farm town? Were they planning to shoot at cows?

Grandma Byrdsong pulled her car to the side and yanked the emergency brake as the trucks rumbled past, and behind them the soldiers. Somehow, the men didn't seem so impressive up close, and there were not as many as Daniel had thought. They looked weary and were not so much marching as trudging. More than one relied on a crutch.

He looked to Bridey for an explanation. He assumed that, as the town's one witch (something she neither admitted nor denied), she'd know everything. But she was gawking like a tourist.

Emily, he realized with a start, was no longer in her seat, but huddled beneath the dashboard, with her skinny arms over her head. *That's right,* he thought with a pang, *she's had run-ins with these people before. They arrested her mom.*

"It's okay," he said when the soldiers had passed. "They're gone."

Emily didn't answer. She stayed under the dashboard, and so did not see when Bridey turned off onto a narrow dirt road with a mane of brown grass running down the middle. She didn't see the car climbing past elms and elderberry that ran leafy hands and scratchy fingernails along the roof and passenger side. Nor did she see the house emerging at the top in dilapidated grandeur, with circle drive and porticoed entrance; or the wild vegetable garden; or the big lilac tree that reached past the second floor; or the cats, some rumored to be feral, peering out from under the rotted porch.

"Here we are," called out Grandma Byrdsong, lurching to a stop. "Home sweet home."

※

Late that night, Emily was wakened by the wind, or was it a sound within the wind? It seemed like a high, soft moaning, more like a call than a moan.

Her grandmother had given her the bedroom at the top of the house, the Four Seasons room, just below the widow's walk. It was a small and private place, square as a box, with a window on each wall, inviting weather from all directions, and a different season from each side. Just now, the window on the summer side was shuddering in its loose frame.

The house, once quite grand, was so full of creaks and groans it was hard to tell where any particular sound was coming from. Seen from the front, the dirty white columns and sagging Victorian trim gave the place the look of a failed wedding cake.

Emily didn't mind. After her days on the road, she was glad for any roof over her head, and this one, at least, didn't leak. It helped to remember that this had been her mother's room once. She lay listening in the darkness. The wind, yes, but there was something besides the wind. Quietly, as if not to frighten the sound away, she slipped from bed and padded barefoot into the hall.

Nothing.

Almost nothing.

She noticed a round-topped door to her left. As a small child, she used to be frightened of it and never tried to get it open. Medieval-looking, heavy and darkly studded, it warned her away. That didn't stop her now, though it took all her strength to pull the bolt on a rusty latch. As she'd hoped, stairs led to the widow's walk on the roof of the house. Stepping outside, she was nearly blown off balance and grabbed on to the iron railing to steady herself. It was scary out here, exposed in all directions to the wild night wind, but exciting, too. Overhead, a quarter moon scythed through a tangle of clouds. Below lay the woods, like a coverlet, and in the midst of it a ribbon of blackness. She squinted, trying to make it out. Then the ribbon began to glint as the moon broke free of the clouds, and she realized she was looking at water, several streams surrounding a sort of island. Strange, she thought, an island in the middle of a forest. This was probably the only place in town that you could see it from. Her grandmother's house stood on a rise of land, giving a view over the treetops.

She heard it again, a faint call like a woman's voice, and it was coming from the direction of the island. She strained to hear. The tall, vine-covered trees swayed like sad dancers. There! She heard it again. Could almost make out the words.

Her breath caught in her throat. She had heard, had thought she'd heard, a voice calling *Where are you? Where are you?*

The words were lost in the sighing of the trees.

The whole island was moving, the curtain of vines swinging like long dresses. Just for a moment, the dresses swung aside, revealing a pale figure within the gloom. Was it an animal? Could it have been a woman? Too far away to tell.

Emily stood leaning out over the rail, staring and staring, but the vines did not part again. Her throat ached with unshed tears and unsaid words.

"*Mama!*" she cried out suddenly into the night. "*I'm here! I'm here!*"

The Captain
Three

Daniel didn't want to take her, but it was hard to argue about it. The girl had been here three days, had no friends, and appeared to be mute. What would it hurt to have her come along on one of his walks?

It was no good to say that Wesley could just as easily take her. This was a school day for him, and there was even a quiz. Name two cities on the Baltic, that sort of thing. Excuses don't come better than that.

To sweeten the deal, Daniel's mother made two bag lunches and added a couple of fresh-baked brownies wrapped in wax paper. Daniel stuffed everything in his backpack, along with some rope and other supplies for his secret cave.

Well, secret. It wasn't really secret and wasn't much of a cave. It went back ten or twelve feet into the rocky hillside and had a narrow entrance formed by a couple of boulders that at some point, centuries ago, must have rolled against each other. Apparently, other kids had used this cave years before, leaving scratchings and designs on the back wall. Daniel liked to think the marks were ancient petroglyphs left by a long-dead civilization, but the illusion was hard to maintain when you saw MOLLY ♥ PETE and HOWIE IS A BIG FAT JERK.

Sometimes he and Wesley built a fire there and camped out, but more often, Daniel went alone to think. He didn't like the idea of taking a stranger with him, but somehow without knowing or even liking her, he trusted this girl. Trusted her silence. She wasn't likely to spill any secrets.

And he had to admit, she'd improved a lot since that first day. A bath and a few nights' sleep had helped; and Grandma Byrdsong had managed to untangle that squirrel's nest of hair. It was still a little on the wild side, but the curls were held firmly in place with a green velvet headband. Standing there in the yard, she looked almost like a regular person, in a simple blue dress with tiny flowers—sleeves to her forearms, and the cuffs fastened with pearl buttons.

It was not a dress to go hiking in, but what would she know about that? She was a city girl, unused to struggling through underbrush or keeping her footing on shale. During the whole time, she didn't say a word.

"Keep up, will you?" Daniel said, seeing her fall behind again. But then he regretted his tone. She was trying. It wasn't her fault she was short and couldn't keep up with his long-legged strides. And how could anybody hike in those shoes? "Come on," he said more gently, "we're almost there."

The hill steepened. Up ahead stood the laurel bushes and the boulders that hid the mouth of the cave. Daniel and his brother had always been careful to vary the way they approached the place, to avoid wearing a path in the hillside that others could see and follow. As a result, there was no easy way to go. Slippery leaves from last year covered unstable stones, and it wasn't long before Emily let out a strangled cry and fell hard.

"Hey," said Daniel, crouching beside her. "Are you okay?" A red spot was visible on her dress near her knee. "Let's take a look at that."

She narrowed her eyes at him.

"Come on," he said. "I'm not going to bite you."

She held the hem of her dress tightly around her ankles. No strange boy was going to look at her knee.

"Have it your way." He stood and pulled her to her feet. "We've got a first-aid kit in the cave. You can use that."

No words. No smile. No complaint, unless you count wincing. They continued on, at last reaching the entrance. He sat her down outside, by the fire pit, and handed her the first-aid kit and his canteen. "Sure you want to do this yourself?"

She didn't look at him.

"Okay. Wash it out really well. Then you can put on the other stuff. I'll be inside."

What a bother she was.

He clicked on his flashlight and headed into the dark to straighten things up: tools, including his coiled rope, on one rock ledge; cans of brown bread and containers of dry food on another; bedrolls up on boards to keep out the damp. As always, he glanced at the "cave paintings" left by former generations of kids. Did they really think they'd fool anyone?

Then came the sweeping out of spiders. That was the part he hated. Spiders gave him a serious case of the creeps.

All this didn't take long, so he counted slowly to twenty. Surely she'd had time enough by now; but when he went back out, she was still fiddling with the bandage. Tears stood in her eyes.

"I see what's the matter," he said, kneeling. "You can't hold the bandage and tie it at the same time. Right?"

She had pulled the hem of her dress down when he appeared, but now, with a sullen look, she raised it a little so he could see.

"Do you mind?" He pulled away the gauze pad. "Did you use the calendula lotion?"

She looked puzzled.

"Here, let me. It'll sting."

Emily bit her underlip when he dabbed the lotion. He bandaged her snugly.

"You okay?"

Slowly she nodded. Her eyes even smiled a little, although her mouth did not.

"Good," he said. "Let's eat."

His mother knew how to make a sandwich, and there was no resisting the brownies. Daniel watched Emily attack her food. Had anyone bothered to teach her manners?

But there was something nice about having her here, someone besides his kid brother, who could never sit still and was always jabbering. Emily certainly didn't jabber. She and Daniel sat on a ledge of rock with their feet hanging down and listened to the wind, which just now was making a magnificent ruckus.

"Ever notice how the wind sounds different in different trees?" he said.

She frowned, listening. Yes, the wind was clattering among the leathery sycamore leaves, gasping through aspens, moaning softly as it passed through the sieve of pines.

They listened for minutes, not saying a word.

"Pretty nice, huh? Want to explore some more? Are you okay to walk?"

A nod.

They headed cross-country, in the direction of the island. There was underbrush to fight through and stands of thorn-studded trees to get around, but eventually they found the path that led to a humped footbridge over a brook.

Emily climbed the cross stays and straddled the bridge's railing, her eyes eager. There it was, not twenty yards away, the island she'd seen from the top of her grandma's house—part of it, anyway.

"You look like you know this place," said Daniel, squinting up at her where she sat.

She wasn't listening. She was staring at the wide, slow-moving stream, and beyond to a wall of foliage swaying gently like the breathing of some spellbound beast.

"Look!" Daniel whispered excitedly. "He's there!"

Emily frowned. Then she saw it, the great blue heron with a fish hanging limply from its bill, and her face relaxed. She looked at Daniel and nodded.

"I always think it's good luck when I see him," said Daniel.

She pulled her breeze-blown hair away from her face.

"Beautiful, is he not?" said a man's voice just behind them.

Daniel spun around, startled by the sight of a military uniform, with slashes of gold on the shoulders—the insignia of a captain. The man inside it was on the short side, but you could tell he was all gristle. He was lounging against the opposite railing, his arm draped around a post. His long, carelessly combed black hair (graying at the sideburns) gave him the look almost of a bandit, an effect heightened by the two hyphens of his mustache. It occurred to Daniel that there was something both casual and dangerous about him.

The man launched himself upright. He nodded at the bird. "You don't see creatures like that in the city. Rats maybe. You want him? I'll shoot him for you." Without a word, he unsnapped his holster and took out a heavy-looking pistol, aiming it carefully.

Daniel stopped breathing. He seemed to lose the power of speech. How do you address an officer? How do you tell him that he must *not*, under any circumstance, do what he is about to do?

The captain glanced from the bird to the boy, and from the boy to the stunned-looking girl. "No?" He lowered the pistol. "Okay. Probably no good to eat anyway."

What Daniel was most aware of, besides the flood of relief, was Emily's hand gripping his shoulder hard enough to hurt.

"Thank you," Daniel managed to say.

The captain pursed his lips, making his mustache bristle. "So," he said, "you are one of those nice people who like to look at the beautiful thing and not shoot it."

It was still hard to speak, but, "Yes."

"I too like to look at the beautiful thing." He flashed a bandit smile, revealing a black space where a dogtooth had been. "Unless I can eat it. Then watch out!" He chuckled at his own wit. "By the way, to let you know, my men will be staying here a few more days. The tents have been sufficient till now, but others will be coming, so we'll be putting them up in farmhouses. I see the young lady is looking alarmed at this."

Her grip on Daniel's shoulder was painfully tight.

"Needn't be, miss. We'll be out of your hair in no time." He looked them both over. "Well, my nature lovers," he said, turning to stroll on, as if he had nothing better to do on a Tuesday afternoon, "it's been a pleasure."

Daniel and Emily watched as he headed off down the path.

"Oh!" he said, doing an off-balance pirouette to face them again. "Could you direct me to a person named Byrdsong?"

Daniel felt his chest freeze up.

The man looked from him to the girl. It wasn't hard to read the fear on their faces, and their efforts to hide it. "You know the lady, then," he said.

Daniel nodded.

"And she lives—where?"

"I . . ."

The man crossed his arms and smiled. "Come, now."

The impulse to lie was so strong that Daniel began to feel a headache stirring behind his eyes. He couldn't do it. "I'm afraid to say."

"Afraid? Why?"

"You might hurt her."

"And why would I do that?"

The boy's head was throbbing. "Because you're a soldier and soldiers hurt people."

The captain rested his hands on his hips, as if to settle himself around this concept. "You have an odd idea about soldiers," he said. "Is that what the people around here think?"

Daniel was silent.

"Well, do they?"

A vein in Daniel's forehead was pulsing. He mustn't speak. "They hate you," he blurted.

"Do they really? Good heavens, we mustn't have that! What about you, miss? Is that what you think, too?"

"She can't speak."

"You mean she's mute?"

"I think so."

The captain contemplated them as he might a mildly intriguing math problem. "Well," he said, "I'll just have to ask someone else, won't I?" He flashed that gap-toothed smile. "Unless I just shoot you. Are you good to eat?"

He laughed loudly, and started off again. Daniel watched until he disappeared.

"Scary guy," he said, more to himself than to Emily. "Hard to figure out. Maybe he's not that bad."

Emily slid down from the railing. She looked Daniel in the eye. *Don't trust him,* she said. Simple as that. Three clear words.

"You can talk!"

She turned and looked back at the heron, and the island behind.

Daniel came up beside her. "Does anybody know you can talk?"

She was silent, and Daniel wondered if she was done speaking, like some oracle that delivers a cryptic message and says no more. "Is it easier that way? People don't ask a lot of questions if they think you can't answer."

No answer. Each non-answer she gave was like another question.

"But then why let me in on it?"

She shot him a glance that was so adult it scared him. "Because," she said quietly, "you are dangerous."

"*What?*" Daniel did not have an overly high opinion of himself, but he'd never thought of himself as dangerous.

"You thought Captain Sloper was not that bad. *Not that bad!*" Less than a dozen words, but coming from her they seemed an avalanche.

"You know his name?" he said.

"Not that bad." Her lips tightened around the bad-tasting words. "If you want to get yourself killed, keep thinking that."

Daniel didn't know what to say.

"Also, you can't lie worth dirt."

"I know I can't."

"'They hate you,' you said. Beautiful!"

"I couldn't help it."

"*That's* what makes you dangerous."

Was this the withdrawn, dirt-caked girl he'd seen such a short time ago on the road to town? Where did she get that tongue of hers?

"How did you know his name?"

"He arrested my mother." She had to look down then, because her air of self-sufficiency was starting to get shaky.

"Oh," he said. "But . . ." His thoughts were swirling and not landing anywhere. "Why would he want to arrest your mother?"

"Why do you keep asking all these questions?"

"I'm trying to understand."

"Don't bother," she shot back. "If you want to help, you can get me onto the island."

"This island?"

"This island, yes. Can you help?"

He glanced over at the stern, yellow-eyed heron. It had begun walking away, lifting its legs as if there were something unpleasant underfoot. "Why do you need to go there?"

"I can't tell you."

Daniel was beginning to think he liked this girl better when she didn't talk.

"First of all," she said, "it's none of your business. But mainly, you can't keep a secret."

She had him there. "Maybe I could learn. It's just I get these—"

"Forget it."

"No, really. I get these fierce . . ."

"Don't worry about it. Just tell me how to get to the island."

He frowned. "I've been trying to figure that out myself."

"Do you at least have a rowboat or something?"

"I wouldn't do that."

"Why not?"

"The two times I heard of, something ripped long gashes in the hull before it got halfway across."

"Superstition."

"Then there's the quicksand."

Emily paused. "Anything else?"

"Water snakes. Poisonous."

"You're making this up."

"Want to take a look?"

"You're making this up. I know it."

"Come on."

He led her off the footbridge, through high-climbing brambles that clawed at their ankles and arms.

"Sure you want to do this?" he said when they were halfway there.

"Keep going."

Wincing with scratches, they made it to the edge of the wide, cloudy creek.

There seemed nothing unusual at first, just a lazy stream on a summer day. But soon a ripple appeared, V-shaped, and at its apex a small, pale head. It was moving downstream, and behind it, beneath the surface, was the undulating body of a snake, five feet long at least. Soon another small head appeared, leaving its V-shaped wake. Then another.

As they watched, one swam quite close to the shore, and Emily stepped back with a gasp. "Did you see that?"

"What?"

"Its head! It's not a snake's head! It's human!"

Daniel looked hard. He had only a glimpse, but it was enough. Human, yes, hideously so, with scales instead of hair, and a glaze of hatred in the eyes.

It was true, then, the old story. Maybe all the stories were true. The place was cursed.

When finally they'd fought their way back to the path, Emily stood silent. Daniel could see she was shaken.

"Still want to get onto the island?" he said at last.

"More than ever."

Their eyes met.

"Me too," he said.

Four
Houseguests

Emily hadn't been home more than an hour when three military cars filled with soldiers swerved to a stop in front of the house. She watched from the autumn window, the one just over the porch, as Captain Sloper jumped out. She was able to see him, she knew, only because the window was closed. Plain glass, plain view—in this case a view of the heat-scorched lawn and exhausted roses that seemed to have quit trying.

The captain bounded up the steps. Emily's view was blocked by the porch's overhang, but she heard him rapping on the door. Her first thought: *They're coming for me! They took Mama, and now they're coming for me!*

The door must have opened, because she could hear Sloper's exclamatory voice and a murmured response. She backed away from the window. Soon heavy feet were tramping through the house. Where could she hide?

She dropped down and crawled under the writing desk.

"Emily, dear!" It was her grandmother calling.

"Shh!" the girl hissed under her breath. "Be quiet, Grandma!"

"Come down, Emily, we've got guests."

Is that what you call them?

A minute later, the door opened and Grandma Byrdsong came in, puffing for air, followed by Captain Sloper.

"That's funny," she said.

One of Bridey's cats, her favorite, the white one called Mallow, padded in and went over to the writing desk, where it sniffed at Emily's sock-covered feet.

"There you are!" said Bridey. "What are you doing under there?"

Emily poked her head out, glaring.

"That's the mute girl I saw in the woods," said Sloper. The corner of his mouth played with the idea of a smile. "Hello, mute girl."

"This is Captain Sloper, dear. It seems we're going to have some of his men staying with us for a few days."

The captain cast his eyes around the little room, taking in the vase of roses on the oak bureau, the narrow bed with its colorful coverlet, and the three framed pictures on a shelf. One photo, in a silver frame, caught his attention. It showed a young woman in a flouncy dress, smiling broadly, her hand resting on a horse's mane.

Sloper's eyes focused intently. It was brief, but Emily caught it. A moment later, his face was a mask of mildness.

"Well," he said, turning to Emily. "Cozy room you've got here. A little small for what we want." He turned to Mrs. Byrdsong. "She can hear me, can't she?"

"Oh, she can hear you quite well."

"That's good. I'd feel silly talking to myself." He smiled, the black gap showing where the tooth was missing. "Not that I'm not good company. But no," he said, turning serious. "Those front rooms downstairs will work very well, I think. And the parlor. Several men can park themselves there." He gave a brief nod to Emily, who was still crouched on the floor. "Emily, is it? Nice seeing you again. I'm sure we'll get to be great friends."

The door closed, leaving her alone with the cat.

Dinner that night was not easy. At her grandmother's direction, Emily had rummaged in the storage room to find leaves to extend the dining table. So instead of a cozy dinner for two plus the cats, there was a raucous party of nine, and all the cats were in hiding. There was one nice-looking soldier, a young, sandy-haired private named Martin, who winked at Emily and made her blush; but the others disgusted her. Soldiers who'd never been taught to keep their feet, much less their elbows, off the table took large portions of everything, leaving little for anyone else.

As for washing dishes, they never thought about that, and just as well, considering the willowware cup that one of them had dropped, and the wine glass that another, at the height of an argument, had hurled into the fireplace.

As soon as she could, Emily retreated to her room at the top of the house. Laughter and bumping furniture could be heard below, punctuated by the slamming of doors, but it felt safe here. Safe enough to take out the necklace her grandmother had given her when she'd arrived: a string of strange-looking pearls—not round, but wobbly in shape. They were freshwater pearls (Bridey had explained) from a place with unusual mineral properties. Bridey claimed they were good for purifying water—said she'd used them several times to make cloudy water drinkable. Emily didn't care about that. All she knew was that they had once belonged to her mother. The necklace, in fact, felt warm, as if Miranda had just unclasped it and laid it in Emily's hands.

The girl formed it in an oval on top of the bureau, beside her book of mythical animals. That, too, was a precious object, the only book Emily had brought with her from the city. Her father had given it to her, two years ago Christmas Eve, the night before he disappeared. Who arrests a man on Christmas? She heard later that he'd been an organizer in the resistance movement, but he never mentioned politics to her. He just told her stories at bedtime about nonexistent animals. She knew he was making the stories up, but she half believed those marvelous creatures were real.

Holding the book now, she felt only nervousness. That was because of what her mother had thrust inside it the night of her arrest.

"Don't let them find this!" she'd said.

A moment later, the door had burst open and three soldiers had entered, demanded that Miranda identify herself, and pulled her from the room before she could so much as glance back at her daughter. With her heart gonging in her chest, Emily had watched from an upstairs window as her mother was led outside into the rain-slicked street. There she was questioned by another man, a captain by the look of him, with a pencil mustache. He poked an accusatory finger in Miranda's shoulder whenever he didn't get a satisfactory answer.

It was Emily's first sight of John Sloper.

As for the paper Miranda had stuck in the book, Emily couldn't make sense of it—it was a hand-drawn map on a folded sheet of heavy paper.

She looked around. The deadbolt on her door looked sturdy enough. She carried the book to the bed and climbed up.

She leafed past full-page illustrations of the Hydra, the unicorn, the Gorgon, and varieties of dragons till she came to the intrusively rough document of her mother's. Before opening it, she glanced, as if for permission, at the silver-framed photo on the bookshelf. It was a wonderful picture, taken years before Emily was born, showing her mother as a teenager, squinting happily into the camera while her hand rested on a horse's mane. It steadied Emily to see it.

"Mama," she whispered. "Was that you calling me the other night?"

No answer but a smile.

That and a soft knock on the door. "Emily?"

Her heart gave a jump, but then she realized who it was and hurried to let her grandmother in.

"Mind if I visit?" Still breathing hard from the climb, Bridey Byrdsong hauled herself to the rocking chair and plumped herself down. "I don't expect they'll be here very long," she said.

Emily nodded.

"Until then we'll have to be good little hostesses." She looked at the oaken wardrobe. "Have you had a chance to try on any more of Miranda's things?"

Emily cleared her throat. It hadn't been used much for speaking. "Not yet," she said.

"Not yet! So, you've found your voice!"

"I never lost it."

Her grandmother compressed her lips in a smile. "I didn't think you had. It might be just as well, though, if the others didn't know it."

"That's what I think, too."

"Does anybody else know?"

Emily hesitated. "Just that boy."

"Daniel? That's all right. You can trust him."

"He doesn't seem very smart."

Grandma Byrdsong laughed. "Why do you say that?"

The girl shrugged.

"I think," said the old woman, "you'll find he's plenty bright enough."

"I'm afraid if somebody asks him, he'll just blurt it out."

"Ah. Something to do with his nerves, they say. He can't seem to lie."

"Strange."

"We all have our shortcomings."

They lapsed into silence.

"Grandma? Can I show you something?" She pulled out the crinkly map.

Bridey scanned it. "She gave you this?"

"'Don't let them find it.' That's what she said."

"Good advice."

"Do you know what it is?"

"I ought to. I gave it to her."

Emily stared. "I didn't know you could draw maps."

"I didn't say I drew it." Bridey tucked back a lock of gray hair. "It's something I was given when I was young. I passed it on to her. Now it looks like she's passing it on to you."

"But what is it? What do I do with it?"

"Did your mother tell you anything?"

"About what?"

Bridey nodded slowly, as if deciding something. "I suppose you should know."

Emily looked worried. "Is it very bad?"

"Not bad at all. It's a privilege being a Byrdsong. But there are responsibilities. The map is one of them. It's been passed down, generation to generation."

"Is it that old?"

"Oh, it's old. Not as old as the island itself, of course."

The girl looked confused.

"The island back in the woods here. The map shows how to get to it."

Emily felt her heart beating. "What is it about that place? Why do you need a map? It's right in plain sight."

"Seems that way, doesn't it? But you can't get there without the map. I call it the impossible island."

"Well," she said, "I know it wouldn't be easy, with all those thorns and everything, but . . ."

"It's not the thorns. The island is protected."

"That doesn't make sense."

"Doesn't it? You saw the stream."

"Of course."

"Did you see the snakes?"

"Yes."

Grandma Byrdsong nodded, rocking. "They're almost the only things that can live there. The water is highly acidic. Did you see their heads?"

Emily flinched.

"That's what's left of folks who tried to get there the

wrong way, for the wrong reasons. They say some of them have been circling that island for a hundred years."

"That's crazy." Emily didn't know why she was getting irritated. After all, she'd seen the snakes herself.

"You may be right." The old woman rocked more slowly. "I know they've been there all my life, and I'm no spring chicken."

"Can't anybody get past them? I mean, without this?" She laid her hand on the map.

"Maybe. Why? You thinking of hopping over there?"

"No," the girl said slowly. "It's just . . ."

The rocker stopped. "What are you saying? What have you seen?"

"Nothing. Well, the other night I almost thought . . ."

"Almost thought what?" Grandma Byrdsong leaned forward.

The girl shook her head.

"Emily, I'm your grandmother."

"I know it's crazy, but for a minute I thought . . . Well, I thought I heard a voice calling me. Coming from the island."

"Whose voice, child?"

"But I was wrong."

"*Whose voice?*"

"My mother's."

Bridey stared at the girl. "Oh dear," she whispered. "Not Miranda." She hoisted herself out of the chair and made for the door. "No, no," she murmured to herself. She left without another word.

The Truth
Five

The old Byrdsong manse, though the largest in town, was not the only place where soldiers stayed. A dozen men set up cots in the schoolhouse. A sergeant and two privates stayed with the town pharmacist. Mr. Fish had to put up with an old artillery man and his dog. Even the Olsens, in their trim, recently renovated house off the main street, took in several. Daniel wondered how Melinda Olsen, the class beauty, felt about giving up her pink bedroom to soldiers.

Captain Sloper, with members of his staff, stayed at the Crowleys', taking over the upstairs and sending Daniel and Wesley to sleep in the barn.

The art of conversation died in Everwood that day. No one felt safe to utter an opinion on anything more provocative than the price of soybeans, and even that had its controversial side. But there was plenty of whispering in back rooms and grumbling in barns about what the occupation was really about and where it would lead.

And that was before possessions started disappearing.

Food, of course, but then a farmer's favorite pipe, the pharmacist's supply of painkillers, Mayor Fench's carved mahogany chess set. No one dared complain. There had been, over the years, too many rumors about the behavior of government troops.

That's what made Captain Sloper's show of friendliness so unsettling. He had particularly warmed to Daniel Crowley, starting that first night at dinner. The captain had been sipping liberally from his hip flask of calvados and was in an expansive mood, going on about how beautiful the countryside was and how stupid the inhabitants—"present company excepted." It was amusing, he told Daniel's father, to watch them attempt to mislead him. Even the mayor was hopeless at it. "I asked him where he kept his best bottles of wine and he almost gagged! I'm sure that you, Mr. Crowley, wouldn't hesitate to tell me where you keep yours."

"Your men are drinking it."

"Really!" He narrowed his eyes. "You wouldn't be lying to me, would you?"

"Not at the moment."

"Well, let me know when you do." He took a swig of calvados and glanced around the table. "That goes for those two fine boys of yours." He smiled amiably at Daniel. "You wouldn't lie, would you?"

Wesley stifled a laugh.

"Oh?" said Sloper. "What are you laughing at, young squire?"

Wesley sobered up quickly.

"You're laughing at your brother. Is that because he tells so many lies?"

Again the boy snuffled with tamped hilarity.

"Come, now," Sloper coaxed. "What's funny?"

"He *can't*!"

"Wesley," said Mr. Crowley, "why don't you help your mother bring in the dinner?"

"No, no," said the captain. "This is interesting." He gazed benignly at the boy. "He can't what?"

"Lie!"

"Wesley," said his father sternly, "that's enough!"

"Let him go on."

But Wesley, suspecting he'd gone too far, was quiet. The captain turned to Daniel.

"Is this true? How do you know you can't lie?"

Daniel gave his brother a dirty look. "Headaches," he said, finally.

"Headaches."

Daniel nodded. "And sweating. Can't catch my breath."

"Nonsense. All boys lie."

Neither brother spoke.

"A boy who doesn't lie is like a dog that doesn't bark," said Sloper. "Let's test it out. Tell me, Daniel, where does your family keep their best wine?"

"Your men are drinking it."

"Bad question. All right, where does your mother keep her best jewelry?"

The boy sighed. "There's a hidden shelf behind the bathroom mirror."

Gwen Crowley had just come in with a platter of meat, and she almost dropped it on the floor.

Sloper glanced from son to mother. "Well, that's the

truth, anyway. I like this boy. He really is the dog that doesn't bark. So tell me. What do you think of Bailey here?" He gestured across the table at a lieutenant, one of his closest aides.

"What do I think of him? I don't know him."

"True. But from what you observe."

"His jokes aren't funny, and it's embarrassing the way he's always flattering you."

Lieutenant Bailey, an expressionless man with calculating eyes, stood up suddenly, his fork gripped in his fist.

"And he scares me," Daniel added.

Sloper clapped loudly. "Well said, boy. He scares me sometimes, too. Oh, sit down, Bailey, for heaven's sake." He shook his head. "Yes, I like this boy."

The captain proved it the next day and in the days that followed, taking Daniel along on jaunts through the countryside, or through the old part of town, like a tourist relying on a guide. It made Daniel nervous to be singled out this way, but his afternoons were never boring. It was impossible to trust the man, but he was more interesting to talk to than, say, Wayne Eccles or Miss Binchey, the postmistress. There was something conspiratorial about the way he looked at you that drew you in, as if the world were a private joke that only you and he were in on. Of course, he was half-drunk much of the time.

"How come he doesn't take me?" said Wesley.

"I guess you're the dog that barks."

"Whaddya mean? I don't bark."

"I'm just saying he can't be sure you'll tell him the truth."

"That's not fair."

"Believe me, I'd rather be you."

One day, the captain let Daniel climb up and take a look inside the tank. The lieutenant who accompanied them gave the captain a warning look.

"What is it, Bailey?"

"Captain," said the soldier, curving a couple of fingers over his mouth as if to keep the wrong people from hearing, "why would you let the townspeople see how the tank works?"

"Because it *pleases* me, Bailey. Besides," he said, "I'm not showing the townspeople, I'm showing Daniel."

Bailey's eyebrow rose fractionally.

"I trust this boy," the captain went on. "More than I can say for most of you."

Daniel looked down and smiled. He descended the metal steps into the machine's steel belly. It took four men to run it, Sloper explained, and yet, except for the driver's stool, mounted on top of the motor, there was nowhere to sit. The viewing slits were narrow, restricting the gunner's vision. But Sloper was proud of his "big pig," as he called it, although it hadn't been used yet in the current conflict and still needed work. He was convinced no enemy could stand against it. Daniel, who'd never seen a machine larger than Wayne Eccles's tractor, was impressed. He also took as many mental notes as he could keep in his head.

The captain was curious about everything. On passing the school, he wanted to know how long the principal had held her position and what the students were taught about the Uncertainties. He took Daniel into the lending library to see what books were on the shelves and was particularly interested to discover several volumes on the use of explosives, although the books hadn't been taken out for years.

Daniel wasn't stupid. He knew he was being pumped for information, the important mixed in with the trivial. But he felt he was learning as much about the captain as the captain was learning about the town.

Anyway, he wasn't really giving away secrets—he had none to tell. The farmers had better things to do than hatch plots behind the hay bales. There were cattle to bring in, fences to repair, corn and soybeans to harvest. They were disgruntled, but not disloyal. Disgruntlement was a local pastime, one of the few. Surely a man of Sloper's intelligence could see *that*.

But maybe he didn't. That would explain his overreaction to an incident involving a piglet.

A man named Hargreave, a reclusive type who didn't care for people much, eked out a bare living from his stony fields up on the west ridge. His neighbors didn't like him any more than he liked them. They used to say his personality was like the smell that lingered on his seldom-washed clothes. But there was one thing he had, a really remarkable sow. He treated that pig better than his wife, and last spring the sow had delivered a fine brood of piglets.

Daniel tried to warn Sloper not to expect a friendly welcome when he went to see about the pigs, but that didn't stop the captain.

"Don't got no piglets," said Hargreave tersely.

"That's not what I heard."

"Sold 'em all. So if you don't mind gettin' off my property . . ."

Sloper sent a man around to the pigsty. He came back holding a little pink squealer. That's when Hargreave reached for his shotgun and ordered the soldiers off his land.

Daniel winced when the old man was disarmed and horsewhipped, each stroke raising a stinging welt. Hargreave seemed determined not to cry out, but by the end he couldn't help it.

"What's the matter?" the captain said, looking over at Daniel. "Think I'm too hard on him?"

"He's just trying to protect what's his."

Sloper stepped into the backseat of the staff car. "I could put up with that," he said, "but not his lying. I had enough lying growing up."

Daniel stepped in after him. "Who lied to you?"

"My old man." Sloper shook his head, remembering. "It wasn't just me; he lied to everyone. He had a real talent." As the car started off, Sloper watched the farmer's wife lead Hargreave into the house. "That's what I like about you," he said. "You can't help telling the truth."

"It's not much fun," Daniel said.

"I suppose not." They rode in silence. "Better than lying, though. I could have turned out like my dad. Thank God for the military. Structure. It saved my life."

Daniel was silent.

"What is it?" said Sloper.

"I don't want to say."

"But I want you to. That's why you're worth my time."

Daniel shot him a glance, unsure what the captain's reaction would be. "What you call structure," he said, "I'd call cruelty."

"Would you, now?" Sloper replied calmly. "An interesting thing, cruelty. Sometimes it's the only way to get people's attention. That pig farmer will think three times before he lies to me again."

The next day, Sloper got everybody's attention. He'd concluded from his experience with Hargreave that farmers in general were not to be trusted with firearms, and he ordered all citizens of Everwood to turn in their guns. They'd be kept safely locked away until the soldiers left town, at which time the weapons would be returned.

Many people chose to hide their firearms rather than give them up. This led to house-to-house searches and more horsewhippings. Being Sloper's guide and counselor was not a job that would make a boy popular, and Daniel did his best to be less available, pleading the need to do chores at home. He'd been putting them off for days.

Sloper gave him one of his looks. "You're trying to avoid me, are you not, little man?"

It would have been so easy for most people to deny it. "Yes, sir," said Daniel.

"Honest to the end."

Daniel looked down.

"Very well," said Sloper, "but I reserve the right to call on you again. I get mortally tired of being lied to."

And so, for the next few days, Daniel was permitted to catch up on chores and even to find some time to himself.

One afternoon ten days after the soldiers had arrived in town, Arnold Fish ambled over to the Crowley place and watched Daniel splitting kindling out back. He stood silently, his snake tattoo bulging. Daniel pretended not to notice him at first, but finally looked up.

"Do me a favor?" said the big man.

"Sure." Daniel ran the back of his hand across his forehead.

"Help me build a coop?"

Daniel looked puzzled. Fish was a morose and mostly silent man who never asked for anything. And then to say something so bizarre . . .

"Don't you already have a chicken coop?"

"Yeah." Fish spat on the sawdust-covered ground. "I need one they don't know about."

Daniel understood what "they" meant. "I'd think I would be the last person you'd ask."

"Why's that?"

"You know."

"You mean not lyin'? That's foolishness. Just takes practice, is all. Everybody can lie. Truth is, there's nobody else I *can* ask. They're all spooked about the soldiers. Bunch of cowards, you ask me."

Daniel could understand. Nobody wanted to get on Sloper's bad side. "When would you need me?"

"Now would be good. While nobody's around."

Daniel leaned his ax against the chopping log.

Fish led him on a walk across two fields to a dip in the land that was out of sight from the road. He had poles and chicken wire and a post-hole digger out there already.

"We got to make it tight," he said. "There's lots of vermin out here."

Fish called anything "vermin" that attacked his chickens. Mostly foxes and hawks, although he might include soldiers on the list.

Over the next several hours, Fish didn't say much, but then he never did. Daniel learned that his neighbor was hoping to hide two dozen hens from the soldiers. More than that would be noticed.

It was hard work, and when they finished, they went back and forth hand carrying cages of squawking birds. By the time they'd set out the feed and water in the new coop, the sun was casting long shadows across the fields.

"Well, son, that's about it."

Daniel nodded.

"Another week, the way these soldiers have been eating, I'd have been cleaned out."

"Glad to help."

"I won't forget it."

If you knew Fish, you'd understand what a compliment this was. It made Daniel smile all the way home.

Bounce

Six

Earlier that day at the Byrdsong manse, Emily was learning a lesson of her own about soldiers. She'd just caught one of them in her room going through her bureau. Ordinarily, she'd be afraid, even terrified, but on this day she was too angry to think straight. Wordlessly she ran at him, pummeling him with her fists. He was so surprised he backed away, half laughing, half afraid of this silent violence.

"Okay, okay! Hey! Cut it out!"

She pushed at him, as if pushing a car out of a ditch, and kept shoving until he was out of the room. It was only after she'd shut and locked the door that the trembling overtook her and she had to sit down, overcome by the enormity of what she'd done.

Through it all, as out of control as she'd appeared, she had not spoken a word. Somewhere in the back of her brain she'd remembered that advice of her grandmother's: "It might be just as well if the others didn't know."

The map at least was safe. At Grandma Byrdsong's

urging, she'd hidden it in another season—in last spring, in fact. Emily was amazed at how easily it was done. Just open the spring window, wrap the map in oilcloth against the weather, and set it on the sill. The map then ceased to exist in the present.

Getting it out again could be a little tricky. First you had to remember whether you'd hidden it in last spring or in next spring. There were two cranks, one on each side of the sash, and either would open the window; but one turned clockwise, and the other counterclockwise. Turn the wrong one and there'd be no map, and a whole different set of birds.

During the afternoons when no one was around, Bridey had showed the girl features of the house she'd need to be careful about. Some were "improvements" Bridey had made herself, like the red leather wastebasket that always looked empty, because whatever you put in it would disappear forever. Obviously, you had to be careful what you threw away. They'd lost one of the cats that way. It had scampered across the sofa and jumped in. They kept a book over the top now.

Other features had always been there, like the hidden staircase on the second floor that led only upward, and yet it let you out in the downstairs hall. The architect, Bridey explained, was her great-granduncle Jakob Byrdsong, who'd spent years developing what he called "impossible shapes" and then applied his discoveries to his house designs. It was a good thing he'd been financially independent, because his work was never in demand.

"An amazing man, Uncle Jakob," said Bridey. "He died before I was born, but I've heard the stories."

"What stories?"

"Oh, many, and they can't all be true. They say when he was a young boy he had a dog named Bounce. He was very fond of this dog. One morning, the servants found Bounce lifeless on the straw mat where he always slept. They went upstairs to tell young Jakob the terrible news, only to find *him* lifeless as well, not a breath in his body."

"How awful!"

"His parents were crying and trying to wake him, but they weren't able to. Just then, the story goes, the dog comes trotting into the room, tail wagging like anything. He goes up to the boy and nuzzles him. And Jakob wakes up! Everybody's amazed. They ask him what happened, and he says, 'I was playing all night with Bounce—on the island!'"

Emily gave her grandmother a serious look. "Do you believe that story? That he could leave his body like that?"

She smiled. "I think if anybody could do it, he'd be the one. Oh, here. You remember the library. Have you seen it since you've been back?"

The girl remembered many things from her early days there, but she hadn't known about others. Back then, she'd taken all the oddities of the house for granted. Only now, seeing through older eyes, did a word occur to her. "This place is magic, isn't it, Grandma?"

Bridey gave her a serious look. "Come. Let's have some tea."

When they were quite sure they were alone, they sat in the library and waited while the blackberry tea finished steeping.

"You're the last of the line," Bridey said. "There's something you need to know about us." She bit into an almond cookie. "We Byrdsongs are protectors," she said.

Emily looked confused.

"It's our nature. It's what we do." Bridey held the top of the teapot with a finger and poured out two cupfuls.

"I don't understand. Protect who?"

"Not so much *who* as *what*. For hundreds of years now, Byrdsongs have protected the island."

"But . . ." Emily stared at her steaming cup. "Why does it need protection?"

"I don't have an answer to that, but look around you. Imagine if the wrong people got over there."

The image of Captain Sloper flew into Emily's mind. His little mustache and cruel eyes.

"The world's gotten coarser," her grandmother continued. "You yourself know about the Uncertainties. The madness is all around us. It's at our doorstep, right in the house, with its feet up on the table."

Emily was surprised at her grandmother's intensity, but more, her clarity. She'd always thought of the old lady as lovably dotty.

"Grandma," she said, "what *is* the island?"

"Ah, that is easier seen than explained."

"You mean I can *go* there?"

"You're a Byrdsong, aren't you? You've got a map, don't you?"

Emily jumped up and hugged the old woman around the neck.

The two of them shared a look brimming with conspiracy. "Grandma," the girl said, "have you ever been there?"

Bridey lowered her voice. "Each of us in the bloodline has to make the trip. I wasn't much older than you my first time."

"What's it like, Grandma?"

Bridey waved the question aside. "You'll find out. The trick is getting there."

"There's the map."

"Knowing how to *use* the map, dear, that's the tricky bit."

"Oh?"

"Think of the windows in your room. That will help you. And you'll need some dirt, of course."

"Dirt, Grandma?"

Bridey saw Emily's look of incomprehension. "You're a smart girl. You'll figure it out just fine."

"Do you really think I will?"

"I have every confidence."

Later, while her grandmother was upstairs napping, Emily wandered around the house by herself, looking into everything. It seemed always to be speaking under its breath, creaking and muttering when the wind was blowing and sometimes when it was not. It was as if the whole place was alive, and her grandmother was the beating heart within it. No wonder Emily loved her.

She loved her almost as much as she hated the soldiers.

Seven
Superstition

The soldiers were easier to put up with at Daniel's house. Captain Sloper and his aides may not have known which side of the plate their fork went on, but they could speak in whole sentences and they told good stories.

Wesley was particularly taken with the soldier talk around him. As the baby brother in the Crowley family, he was drawn to the rough, the tough, and the grown-up. When a big-chested soldier named Crenshaw told of a drunken escapade ending in an overturned truck in a cow pond, Wesley giggled as if he'd been there himself.

Sloper was the most engaging of all. He would tilt his head toward you and lower his voice in a confiding tone, as if you actually mattered.

"John," said Sloper, leaning back in his chair, "how do you manage to get by, with that store of yours, when most of your customers raise crops of their own?"

"I didn't say I was doing well," Crowley said with a smile. "But well enough to raise two hungry boys."

One of the boys, just then, was not very hungry. Daniel was too busy being mortified to have an appetite for corned beef. It embarrassed him that his father was forced to put up with these occupiers, feeding and housing them and answering their questions.

And it bothered him that Sloper wouldn't give an exact date when his troops would be leaving. They'd been here almost three weeks now. "We're awaiting reinforcements," he said with a nodding smile. "There's a platoon a few miles west of here. No," he said, catching Mr. Crowley's look, "you won't have to feed them! When they join us, we'll pack up and head to the city to finish the fight."

Crowley looked thoughtful. "And the fight? It's going well?"

"Splendidly." Sloper tilted back farther and gazed at a corner of the ceiling, as if conjuring visions of victory. "We're in the mopping-up stage now."

"Oh. Mopping up!"

An interesting thing about Daniel was that while he couldn't tell a lie himself, he could usually guess when one was being told. It was something in the eyes. Sloper had said that the fight was going well, and his eyes had darted, for the briefest moment, to the side. Daniel interpreted that to mean the fight was going badly.

He remembered the condition of the troops as they'd marched into town behind the artillery caisson and the line of military cars. The vacant expressions. The listless trudging. The crutches.

If all that was true, what was Sloper so cheery about? He just sat there gobbling his meat and cabbage and asking about the local populace. He said he'd seen a farmer that afternoon sprinkling some sort of liquid outside his barn door. On questioning, the man had said it was pig urine, and its function—

"Yes, yes, I know," said Crowley with a laugh. "It keeps out bad spirits that would sour his milk."

"That's it! Remarkable!" Sloper shook his head. "I have to say, though, he didn't seem very friendly when we spoke to him."

"Oh, he's all right," said Crowley. "I know who you're talking about. Wayne Eccles. A fine man, once you know him."

"I'm sure he is." Sloper tented his fingers. "Not crazy about the government, though. Told us, excuse the expression, to go to hell."

Crowley flicked his hand to dismiss the thought. "That's Wayne for you. But, I mean, who is crazy about the government? Are you crazy about the government?"

"I'm *loyal* to the government."

"Of course. I didn't mean . . ." Crowley felt Gwen's foot kick him under the table.

"Quite all right," said Sloper mildly.

"I mean, nobody likes their taxes raised. Twice in the year."

Another under-the-table kick.

"We're fighting a war, Mr. Crowley. That takes money."

"I understand."

"I'm sure you do." He looked around the table. "I hope Mr. . . . What's his name again?"

"Eccles."

Sloper nodded to his aide across the table. The man took out a small notebook and jotted down the name. "I hope Mr. Eccles understands as well."

The table grew so silent you could hear the candles flicker.

"Captain," said Gwen Crowley, her smile preceding her as she leaned forward, "you needn't worry about the loyalty of the people of Everwood."

"That's comforting to hear, madam."

"They're good, hardworking people. Simple as paint, but loyal as you could ask."

"I'm sure."

One of Sloper's aides snuffled a laugh. "And crazy as magpies!"

"As pig urine!" chortled the one named Bailey.

The captain turned an amused eye to Daniel. "Do you believe in these superstitions?"

The boy, to be honest, wasn't ready to discount them all. "I don't believe in the pig urine," he said at last.

"Good lad."

"Danny, tell him about the island," piped Wesley. "There's all *kinds* of superstitions about that!"

"Wesley," said John Crowley, "the captain is not interested—"

Sloper held up a silencing hand. "Let him speak. What island is this?"

"Well," said Wesley, ignoring Daniel's shut-your-mouth look, "there's all these stories about weird animals that live there."

"Is that right?"

"And there's a gate or a door in the middle of it that leads somewhere. Nobody knows."

"And why is that?"

"'Cause nobody's ever been there."

"Really? Never?"

Wesley shook his head proudly.

Sloper turned to Daniel. "Is that what we saw from the bridge that first day?"

Daniel felt his chest tighten. "Part of it," he said.

"I remember the heron."

"Yes."

"Have you eaten him yet?" Sloper's grin revealed the gap between his teeth.

"Not yet, sir."

"You may have to, with all these soldiers to feed."

"Yes, sir."

"And you say no one lives there?"

Daniel could only shake his head.

"Sounds perfect. And people are superstitious about it—think it's bad luck or something?"

"They're afraid of it."

"Better and better."

The boy tried to read the captain's features, but he could see only contradiction: face mild as mist, eyes stormy with schemes.

"Why are you interested in the island?" Daniel said.

"I'm thinking it might be the perfect place to test our new artillery. You've seen our big pig of a tank. It's finally ready."

"Don't use the island," said Daniel.

Sloper turned his head to the side, as if to hear better. "Why not? The gun's got to be tested. Why not in a place where no one goes, where there are no houses, no crops, not so much as a stray cat?"

"But you can't get to it. It's surrounded by thorn trees and—"

"Perfect! It'll keep people away. I think you'll agree," Sloper said, "it's better than testing it on that fellow's farm. Pig urine!"

Sloper's aides barked with laughter.

Daniel stood, upsetting his glass of apple juice. He didn't notice. "Not the island."

Sloper took this in. "You feel strongly," he said.

"Yes, sir."

"Why?"

Daniel shook his head. Why? He hardly knew himself.

"You must have a reason," Sloper pursued.

"You'll think it's stupid. You'll think I'm superstitious like the farmer who buries a sock in the corner of his field."

"I don't think you're stupid. That's the last thing I think."

"There's just . . . something about it," Daniel managed. "Something untouched. It should stay that way." He didn't know how else to put it. Abashed, he sat down.

"I see." Sloper darted an amused glance at his aide-de-camp across the table. "That *does* make a difference. There's only one thing that puzzles me," he said, stroking his mustache. "Do the farmers around here *really* plant socks in their fields?"

The Thief

At ten the next morning, the roof tiles were already hot, and Emily had brought up a towel to sit on. There was a breeze somewhere—she could see the clouds overhead being cuffed around—but the roof's peak blocked it from reaching her. She'd been up here several times, hoping to hear the voice that had called her from sleep that first night. But the only sounds she heard were the arguments of birds, the laughter of soldiers below, and the twang and slap of a screen door.

From here, the view stretched impressively from the Byrdsong manse to the beginnings of town, with all the barns and fields between. Straight before her lay the forest. She knew where the island was, but it was hard to see in the profusion of foliage. Ah, there was the footbridge she'd stood on with Daniel. Four or five people were there now. Soldiers, pointing and gesturing.

She spread out the map on her knees.

You'll figure it out, Grandma Byrdsong had said, but it was as mysterious as ever. It seemed to mark places, but gave no place names. And it gave no hint of scale. Did it cover miles or only yards?

And what were these markings, nearly illegible with age, around the edge of the map? Some were symbols, while others were clearly (or unclearly) words. "Cover the Serpent," one line began. Emily puzzled over it, squinting in the sunlight. *Cover the Serpent with something something. Next Spring's Earth?* She spoke the words: "Cover the Serpent with Next Spring's Earth."

Now that makes a lot of sense.

There was a second line, ending "for the something Rebirth." The *Heart's* Rebirth? That was it.

Closing her eyes, Emily tried to visualize the island; but all she could think of was the house below her, its spiral staircase twisting its way up to the turret and the Four Seasons room.

Just then she heard a familiar sound below her, the honking protest of a heavy drawer being pulled open.

A bureau drawer. *Her* bureau!

The map slid off her knees as she jumped to her feet. She made a grab for it and felt it tear slightly. *Careful*, she told herself. She folded it hastily. A moment later, she was on the stairs, then in her room. Empty. But the top drawer of her bureau was not completely shut. She went over and yanked it open. That same groaning sound. Nothing seemed to be missing.

She rummaged wildly. The small oblong case was still there. But—she snapped it open—the necklace was gone! That pearl necklace had belonged to her mother. Grandma Byrdsong had given it to her that first day in Everwood.

At first, Emily thought her grandmother might still have it. She'd borrowed it yesterday to clear a bucket of water that wasn't quite right for drinking. The water had come from the rain barrel that caught runoff from the roof, and it wasn't always drinkable. Emily had been there with her, watching as the cloudiness dissipated and the water grew clear and sweet. But she remembered distinctly bringing the pearls back up—yes, she had dried them on her blouse—and returning them to their case.

She heard a staff car revving up and pulling out of the gravel drive, and suddenly she was sure who the thief was. It was the same man she'd found in her room the other day, the one with the high, surprised-looking forehead and meaty hands. She raced from the room, her feet pummeling the staircase. She flashed by the kitchen where Grandma Byrd-song and Mrs. Beinemann were sitting with their midmorning tea, and then she was out in the yard by the vegetable garden.

No one in sight. Where would he have gone? She remembered the soldiers down by the footbridge. No reason to think he'd gone there, but it was worth a try. She set out at a run.

A pain in her side soon slowed her to a walk. She was wearing a light sundress of her mother's that she'd found in the closet, but she was still sweating. The pain began to lessen, and she pushed herself to a trot. Finally, practically gasping, she found the footpath that led to the bridge, and the car parked in the grass.

There they were with that bastard Sloper, a clipboard in his hand, taking notes and gesturing with his pencil.

"Ah," he said. "Miss Emily. Well."

Don't speak, the girl warned herself. *Remember.*

She came up to the knot of men. She recognized that

good-looking soldier named Martin who'd smiled at her at dinner. And sure enough, there was the one she was looking for. He looked big, and he looked dumb. His fists were on his hips. Without a word, she dipped her fingers into his shirt pocket.

"Hey!" he yelped.

She reached into his pants pocket next. There it was.

As she pulled out the necklace, the man's heavy hand, unpleasantly warm, clamped down on her. "Whaddya think you're doin'?"

She fixed him with a furious stare as she twisted to get free of him, but he was strong. With all her force, she kicked him in the kneecap, and his grip loosened. All this happened before she had time to think or others had time to react. But the pearls were in her hand, and she danced back, away from the man.

He was after her in a moment and managed to grab her other arm.

Emily was not a large person, but the sound that came from her then was a growl that would have made anyone pause. This man was *not* going to get this necklace!

With a strength she had no idea she had, she pulled back her free arm and hurled the necklace high into the air. It arced over the brambles and baneberry, over the murky stream, and landed on the bank on the other side.

The soldier, outraged, gave the girl a slap that knocked her off her feet and into the bushes beside the bridge.

It took three other soldiers to hold him back from tromping her to death.

"Stop that!" bellowed Sloper.

"That's mine!" cried the thief, pointing at the glimmering necklace across the water.

"I doubt that very much," said the captain. "But you can go over now and get it and bring it back to the girl." He glared at him. *"Go!"*

Breathing hard with indignation, the soldier hulked through the undergrowth, ignoring as best he could the clawing resistance of thistles and brambles. A thorny branch slapped him in the face, drawing blood and oaths.

Emily pushed herself up on her elbows and watched him. She tasted something warm and metallic and realized her lip was bleeding. That didn't stop her from smiling.

Reaching the margin of the water, the man waded right in, his eyes on the circle of pearls on the far bank. He had not gone three strides before he felt his booted feet being slowed by some underwater resistance. With all his strength, he managed a fourth step, sinking from waist to chest, and then could go no more.

Though he thrashed about wildly, his efforts seemed only to pull him deeper. Panicking, he let out an inarticulate cry. The murk was now to his chin, his head tilting back to keep his face from being covered. "For God's sake!" he gargled. "Help!"

Sloper nodded to the soldier named Martin. "The idiot can't swim."

The young man gave a smart salute and trotted ahead, straight into the stinging undergrowth. You could see his suffering as he fought his way forward, but he didn't complain.

Emily winced. The word "No!" escaped her as a whisper.

By the time he made it to the edge of the creek, his arms and one cheek were bleeding freely; but he dove in without hesitation, reaching his comrade just as the man's head was sinking from sight. There was a turmoil as rescuer and rescued struggled together; but it was no use. The first man was firmly stuck, his head now under the water, his arms flailing more feebly as the seconds passed. About then, the other soldier felt the pull of the muck beneath him.

"Quicksand!" he called out. "Help! I can't move!"

He *was* moving, though—downward. Two other soldiers fought through the resistant underbrush, hoping to get close enough to throw their friend a rope. It was all happening too fast. The young man was barely keeping his chin above water.

That's when he saw a delicate V of ripples swerving in his direction. His look of puzzlement turned to horror when he saw it was a snake. He thrashed wildly and sank up to his nose. That left his eyes at water level as the snake reached him, its pale head gleaming, its human eyes brilliant with malice.

Emily, who'd been watching from the bridge, ducked her head to the side to avoid what happened next, but she heard the scream. The mad splashing. The quick intake of breath of the soldier beside her.

A long silence followed. That was worst of all.

Finally, head still down, she dared to look. The water was calm. A finch began to trill atop a thorn bush.

Then she saw it, a sudden presence on the other bank. It was the heron. Slowly, even daintily, it approached the necklace and uncurled its neck. It dipped low to examine the strange object. The long beak pushed it, then opened and picked it up. Straightening, the creature turned its head, flashing one yellow eye and then the other at the soldiers across the stream.

The necklace swung from its beak as the bird walked slowly away.

Nine
Gone

Dinner that evening was quiet at the Crowley house. The captain seemed to have lost interest in the inhabitants of Everwood, including his host. He abruptly excused himself before dessert and went outside, followed by his men, the screen door slapping behind them. Gwen was thrown off by this. She had baked a cherry pie, now cooling in the kitchen. Catching her look, her husband fractionally lifted his shoulders.

If dinner was quiet at the Crowleys', it was stony at the Byrdsongs'. Two empty chairs stood at the end of the table like accusations. The men rifled angry looks at Emily, as if the deaths that day had been her doing.

Even Bridey was quiet. She'd had a bath that afternoon and had learned more than she'd cared to know. Later Emily helped her with the dishes in the kitchen. The water had been brought in earlier from the well and heated on the stove. Now it was poured into two basins, one with soapy water, the other clear for rinsing, with a lantern above them hanging on a nail.

Emily was struggling to open the grease jar.

Her grandma smiled. "You'll never get it that way."

"What do you mean?"

"Righty tighty, lefty loosey."

Now the girl really didn't understand.

Bridey made a little circle in the air with her finger. "The other way. Counterclockwise."

"Ah." The top screwed off easily.

The old lady gave her one of her pay-attention looks. "You'll want to remember that."

"Righty tighty."

"Lefty loosey, yes. Don't laugh."

Emily shrugged. "I guess you heard what happened today," she said.

"Why don't you tell me?"

As they finished drying the pots, Emily told her grandmother the details. The old lady looked grim but not surprised. The suds had shown her two soldiers fewer. They'd also told her the map was in danger.

"Is it still hidden in last spring?" Bridey asked.

"No, I took it out to look at it."

"Where did you put it, dear?"

"Oh!" Emily said, realizing. She fished it out of the pocket of her dress, rumpled and slightly torn.

"Is this how you take care of things?"

"I'm sorry. I forgot about it."

A male voice interrupted. "Forgot about what?"

Emily whirled around to face John Sloper, lounging against the doorway. He saw Emily's quick movement. "I'll take a look at that, if you don't mind."

Emily held the paper behind her.

"Now that we know you can talk."

Emily flushed. There went two secrets in a single moment.

Sloper's hand was out.

"It's mine!" Emily said.

"Nonetheless." The hand remained extended, and Emily finally brought out the map. The captain went over to a hanging lamp where the light was better. "What is this?"

"I don't know," Emily said honestly.

"Then why do you have it?"

Bridey spoke up. "Didn't you ever make treasure maps when you were a boy?"

Sloper gave her a look that said *This is not worthy of you.* "I didn't make them on hundred-year-old parchment."

"What makes you think it's anything like that old?"

"Seventy or eighty, then. I wouldn't put it at a day less."

Bridey sighed. "No," she said, "you were right the first time."

He frowned at the document. "So what is it?"

"It's a family thing. Nothing that concerns you."

"Well," said Sloper, waving the page in the air, "maybe it's your family that does concern me. Your daughter, Miranda, for instance. A traitor with the rebels."

"Oh, please."

"They loved her. They took inspiration from her. She even sang to them."

"Where did you hear such nonsense?"

Emily's eyes flitted back and forth between the grown-ups as if watching a tennis match. Tennis with an explosive ball.

"She has confessed as much."

Point to Sloper.

"What have you done with Miranda?" said Bridey quietly, the hint of a quaver in her voice.

"We put a few questions to her."

"And she answered them? Just like that?"

"Not just like that."

Bridey stared into the sink. The soap bubbles covering the dishes had no wisdom to offer. "Did she tell you about this?" She nodded at the map.

"We didn't know about it, so we didn't ask. But I'm asking now."

"And I'm telling you it has nothing to do with your ridiculous wars. You yourself can see it's much older than the Uncertainties."

Sloper turned the page back and forth, considering. "True, the parchment is old. That doesn't mean the writing is."

The woman had no answer.

"For all I know, it could show the location of weapons caches. Or meeting places. Putting it on parchment could be a ruse."

Bridey leaned against the sink. She wasn't used to standing up so long and her legs were aching. "Captain, that's farfetched, and you know it."

"If it's not subversive, why won't you tell me what it *is*?"

"I have another idea. Why don't you tell me where Miranda is?"

His face reverted to casual. "Maybe we can work out a trade. I'll tell you if you tell me."

"I don't think so."

"But why not?"

"Because, Captain, it is none of your business."

Sloper's body tightened. "You're a reckless woman, Mrs. Byrdsong, and I can see you don't care about what's good for you. I wonder if you'd be so reckless about your granddaughter here."

Bridey's nostrils twitched.

"I have a feeling," he said, "you'd do just about anything to keep her safe."

"Now, Captain." She attempted a little laugh. "This is all silly. You can see what it is yourself! It's just a map of the local towns, and there's Everwood in the middle. See?" She held the back of a kitchen chair for support.

He scanned the page. "I see that it could be."

"It is. It obviously is."

"What's not obvious," he said, "is why you wouldn't say that in the first place."

"Pure contrariness."

"I think there's more to it. What are all these little signs and symbols? And there are words around the border. Something about a serpent? I can't make it out."

She peered at it. "You'd have to ask my ancestors."

"I'm asking you!"

"I think I'll let you figure it out yourself."

"Don't mock me, old woman," he said. "You do not want me for an enemy."

"I'm sure, Captain Sloper," she replied, lifting her head grandly, "I don't want you any way at all."

"Well." He tucked the document into an inside pocket. "In that case, I bid you good night."

It wasn't the crickets that woke Daniel late that night; it was their sudden stop. He sat up in his sleeping bag.

"Hello?" he called in a whisper. "Who's there?"

Who is *ever* there, when you wake in the darkness, with your heart beating?

He remembered now that he was not in his room but in the hayloft beside his sleeping brother. They'd been banished to the barn for the duration. That was fine with him. The less he had to do with Sloper and his men, the better.

That didn't explain the strangeness. The world seemed the reverse of its familiar, daytime self, like the back of a mirror, showing him not the friendly objects of his daily life, but a dull blankness.

Something, someone was absent. A mirror had gone dark. A sound had ceased.

But the crickets. Why had *they* stopped? That suggested a presence, not an absence. A prowler?

Carefully, so as not to waken Wes, he extricated himself from the sleeping bag and climbed down the ladder from the loft. Moonlight leaked through the old wall boards, throwing stripes of light across the barn floor where Daniel sat lacing his sneakers. A sudden thud from one of the stalls made him jump, but it was just Nate, the Crowleys' horse, shifting in his sleep.

The big sliding door gave a groan as Daniel pushed it open a few careful inches. He considered lighting the lantern that hung from a nail, but there was no need, with the bright half-moon in a cloudless sky. Anyway, why alert any intruders who might be out there? Unlikely, he thought, but *something* had silenced the crickets.

He peered across the stretch of broken ground at his family's house, its roof gray-silver in the strange light. How quiet was too quiet?

He stepped out. The moon shone like a spotlight, frosting the tops of trees and throwing their undersides to blackness. Daniel slid into the shadows, becoming a shadow himself.

Nothing.

Something in the nothing. He held his breath, the better to hear, but the only sound was his heart bashing away in his chest.

A sudden scuttle of leaves behind him made the hairs rise on the back of his neck. The next moment, a hand grabbed his shoulder, and he let out a strangled cry.

"Shh!" hissed a voice.

His eyes began to adjust. "You!"

"Who did you think?" whispered Emily.

The girl, as she emerged more clearly, looked shaken herself. "I didn't mean to scare you," she said, "but I didn't know who else I could trust."

"What is it?" he said.

"It's Grandma."

"What about her?"

She looked around as if there were spies out there in the dark.

"Emily, what happened?"

"She's gone!"

Ten
Sloper by Moonlight

Daniel led the girl to the barn and slid the door shut behind them. He lit the kerosene lamp, turning the wick low. "Now," he said as they sat cross-legged on the floor with the lamp between them, "tell me what happened."

"Tell me, too," piped a voice from above. It was Wesley, starting down the ladder.

"You know my brother," said Daniel.

The girl looked at Wesley's eager ten-year-old face. "Hi," she said without enthusiasm.

"Hey." Wesley plunked down beside his brother. "What's up?"

"Is it okay to tell him?" said Daniel.

Emily sighed. "Sure."

"Well," said Daniel, "Grandma Byrdsong has disappeared."

"Wow," said Wes. "Just like Mr. Eccles!"

Everybody had heard about Wayne Eccles. The old farmer had said something unpleasant to Captain Sloper, and yesterday he'd disappeared. There weren't that many places he could go, unless he'd slunk out of town, abandoning farm and family. That wasn't Wayne.

Emily bit her lip. "I don't know. Tonight she had an argument with Sloper."

"Your grandmother? What about?"

She wasn't sure how much she should say with Wesley there, but it couldn't be helped. "It was about a map. One my mother gave me." She was surprised to find her voice suddenly shaky. Tears filled her eyes.

"Hey," said Daniel softly.

"That must be one important map," said Wesley.

"All I had left of my mother was that map, and she begged me not to let the soldiers find it. And now, because of my own stupidity . . ." Her voice twisted in her throat.

The boys were quiet. They hadn't had much experience with someone breaking down like this.

"Can you tell us about it?" Daniel said at last.

She wiped her face with the back of her hand. Haltingly she told them what her grandmother had said, that it was the only way onto the island.

"A treasure map?" said Wesley hopefully.

"You'd like that," said his brother.

"Don't think so," she said. "But the way Grandma was talking, it sounded like the most important thing in the world."

"What do you know about the island?" Daniel said.

"Nothing for sure. But that first night . . ." She took a big shuddering breath. "That first night I was on the roof and I thought I heard something."

"Heard what?"

"A voice. Coming from the island."

"But nobody *lives* there," Wesley piped up. "Nobody can *get* there!"

"Did you recognize the voice?" Daniel pursued.

Emily looked from Wesley's eager face to Daniel's sober one. "It sounded like a woman. It sounded—" she began, but then stopped herself. "Never mind."

They were all silent. There was a lot of darkness in the barn surrounding the little circle of light, and the three kids huddled in its glow.

"I can't think that Bridey was trying to get to the island," said Daniel. "She can hardly walk!"

"Well, she's out there somewhere," said Emily.

"Know what I think?" he said. "I think we should wake everybody up. The whole town. Get them all looking."

"There's the bell in the church," said Wesley, jumping up. "We can start by ringing that!"

"We should tell Mom and Dad first," said Daniel.

"What about the sheriff?" Wesley said.

"Bingham? He hasn't been exactly . . ."

"I know. Good thing we don't have much crime in Everwood."

It was true. Fred Bingham was a beet farmer who'd taken the side job as town sheriff because it involved almost no work and no one else wanted it. It strained his capacity to get a cat out of a tree.

"Probably we should tell the mayor, too," Wesley said.

"Fench? Maybe."

"Do whatever you want," said Emily, "but do it soon!"

The bell was deafening, loud enough, as they say, to wake the dead. So it seemed to the three kids standing beneath it, yanking on the rope with all their might. It was certainly loud enough to wake the citizens of Everwood. People came from all directions, some of them running, several carrying buckets of water, expecting fire.

Daniel couldn't hear at first—his ears were ringing. It wasn't until he'd gotten outside, in front of the forming crowd, that his hearing was mostly back. He stood on the top step with Wes and Emily. Sheriff Bingham was making his way up to join them. Mayor Fench was coming, too, tucking in his shirttails.

"This better not be a prank," said a farmer near the front.

"Do they know what *time* it is?" said his nightgowned wife.

"We're sorry to get you all out here," Daniel called over their heads, "but there's an emergency. You all know Bridey Byrdsong. Well, she's disappeared!"

"What did he say?" growled Mr. Fish, who had heard perfectly well. "Bridey the witch?"

"She can't walk very well." Daniel looked out over the crowd. "And her car's still in the garage."

The mayor and the sheriff stood conferring, then Sheriff Bingham stepped forward. He lifted his head, looking as sheriff-like as possible. "We had search parties out looking for Wayne Eccles today," he announced loudly. "We're going to have to call on you again tonight. Do we have enough lanterns?"

"We have some in our basement," called out Fish's wife, Min.

"We do, too," said Gwen Crowley, toward the back of the crowd. She gave her boys an encouraging half wave.

"Good! Meanwhile, let's split up into groups of five."

Mayor Fench then had "a few words" to say. The people of Everwood knew what that meant and began to disband. Some older townsfolk headed back to bed, but most wanted to join the search. They might make fun of Bridey, amused at her forgetfulness or her unique approach to driving; but they liked her, even those who secretly believed, or hoped, she might be a witch.

Suddenly Captain Sloper roared up in his staff car, jumped out, and strode through the crowd, followed by several aides.

He seemed not to notice Sheriff Bingham's presence as he turned and surveyed the people.

"I hear an old lady's gone missing," he called out in a voice that echoed back from the building across the street. "We're here to help."

Several farmers exchanged looks.

"What's the matter?" Sloper barked. "Come on! Get moving. Time's wasting!"

✻

Everyone assumed that Grandma Byrdsong could not have gone far, so mostly they stayed close by the house, their lanterns making an irregular necklace around the yard and outbuildings. The soldiers, meanwhile, rummaged around inside, from the root cellar to the Four Seasons room in the turret. One soldier was seen waving his lantern from the widow's walk.

The Crowley boys and Emily concentrated on the wooded hill that slanted down from the house. If Bridey had slipped, or been pushed, they might find her there. How could someone like Bridey Byrdsong, a person of such weighty presence, become an absence?

Daniel didn't think she could. He suspected that Captain Sloper knew exactly where she was—which meant that all this searching was just a charade.

And there the captain was, standing on the rise, a black cutout against a brilliant half-moon.

Could he really be that cruel?

Could he really have killed Bridey Byrdsong?

The Map

"Why don't you keep searching around here?" Daniel whispered, handing Emily the lamp. "I need to check on something at home."

She gave him a questioning look. "Now?"

"What's up, Danny?" said Wes.

"Just something I need. I'll find you," he said, and disappeared into the shadows. He hadn't wanted to worry them; but this was the perfect time, while Sloper was busy at the Byrdsong place, to go back and search for that map of Emily's.

Daniel walked his bicycle across the yard, keeping away from the road till the house was out of sight. Then he jumped on and pedaled like mad. The wind was picking up, swinging from tree to tree, passing him, doubling back, arguing in the branches overhead.

He arrived in a sweat and left his bike in the shadow of the barn, approaching his house from the rear. An old staff car was parked outside. That made him stop, listening hard;

but he couldn't hear anything over the racket of crickets and the sirens of cicadas.

There was a light in the kitchen, so he circled around to the front and entered there, easing the screen door closed. The place seemed deserted, except for a second lieutenant banging about making coffee in the kitchen. He didn't notice Daniel steal past, avoiding the squeaky stair as he climbed to the second floor.

On the landing, Daniel had the advantage of a carpet (worn as it was) to muffle his approach to his bedroom. Sloper's room now.

He lit the kerosene lamp and looked around. It gave him a queer feeling to see the place in such a mess, almost as if it had been burglarized. Sloper might be a disciplinarian with his men, but he'd never been taught, apparently, to straighten his room. An undershirt and a forlorn brown sock lay over the bookcase. A cartridge belt curled on the floor at the foot of the unmade bed. Along the window ledge, Daniel's collection of tin knights and armored horses was in disarray.

Where, in this chaos, would the captain hide a map?

Daniel knelt beside an open duffel bag, going through it slowly, finding clothes mostly, but also a journal and several books. But no loose papers. Certainly no map.

Carefully he began putting things back. He was about to set the journal where he'd found it, but hesitated. It was of mottled leather, badly scuffed. This might be important, the captain's private thoughts. Surely it wouldn't hurt to peek?

Actually, it did hurt, or was beginning to. Daniel might justify looking into a man's diary, but his nervous system wasn't going along. To his brain, it was too much like lying.

His skin had a prickly feeling, and pain signals began zipping along neural pathways, making Daniel wince his eyes shut.

Still, why not a quick look? He'd need to do it before the throbbing in his head became intolerable.

He leafed to the most recent page, and the words "kicking myself." He read on. "Hate to admit I was taken in by that rustic act of theirs. Just simple farmers, stumbling over their dung heaps. All the while . . ."

Daniel closed his eyes tight and massaged his temples. The pain was sharp and getting sharper. He glanced at the page, scanning the last sentences. "All the while plotting and scheming. The old lady's worst of all. See how these traitors feel when we leave, and there's not one stick left standing, nor by God one stone on top of another."

Daniel slapped the journal shut, sweat beading his forehead, his stomach nauseated with pain—or was it fear? He buried the book under some dirty laundry at the bottom of the duffel.

The man's crazy, he thought. *He thinks we're plotting against him, when all the while he's the one . . .*

Daniel *had* to find that map. Whatever it meant, it mustn't be left in Sloper's hands. Daniel tried to think. Maybe the closet? His own clothes, he found, had been pushed aside, and several of Sloper's uniforms and shirts hung in their place. He went through pockets and was peering inside shoes when a whistling sound from downstairs stopped him. The sound started low and rose to a scream, like a hysterical woman. The kettle, he realized.

Daniel went back to work. He'd found nothing and was running out of places to look. He turned finally to his bookcase, to books he hadn't read since childhood, as well as fantasy stories he still liked to read, a dictionary, a math workbook, a history book he needed to return to the library. No map.

But then, in the darkness at the back of the second shelf, he saw the wavy edge of . . . something. An old-looking document on wrinkled brown paper. He pulled it out. Yes, that was it. *Now to get out of here!*

Before he could reach the door, he was stopped cold by the sound of voices downstairs. He edged the door open. The voices were muffled, but there was one he recognized: that soldier with the cold eyes and cautious voice—Sloper's aide, Bailey.

"Got a cup for me?" he was saying.

An indistinct response.

"Can't stay," the first voice continued. "The captain wants me to check if the old lady's turned up."

"Not here."

A grunted reply. Then: "How can you drink this stuff?"

"Hey, nobody's making you."

A kitchen drawer banged shut, rattling silverware.

"Who cares about old Birdbrain anyway?"

"The captain. Don't ask me why."

"He didn't care about the farmer we dumped in the creek."

"Yeah, well."

There was a scrape of a chair, followed by the bang of the flimsy screen door. Then silence.

So, Daniel thought, *Sloper doesn't know where she is, either.* That made him feel better somehow, until he thought about

Wayne Eccles, the missing farmer. *Dumped in the creek!* It made Daniel's chest go cold to think of the snakes.

And there was the journal. *Not one stick left standing.*

He had to get out of here! Just then he heard the lieutenant moving around below. He'd left the kitchen for the sitting room. Daniel was stuck. Nothing to do but hope the soldier didn't suddenly decide to come upstairs.

His heart beating fast, the boy spread the map open. There were words, smudged by age, around the edge, but no place names, just strange symbols here and there, almost like hicroglyphics. He could only guess that the three large patches along the sides of the map were the three neighboring towns, and that the L-shaped section in the center was Everwood.

He looked closer, grateful that his headache was ebbing. In the center of the central area, he saw, lay a smaller patch. Was that the island? There was no indication it was surrounded by water. And what were those symbols? Three little spirals, each a delicate line curling like a snail shell three times in a leftward direction.

The bang of a door made Daniel jump. A decisive voice—Sloper's!—and then boots on the stairs, getting louder.

There was no time to think. Sloper was coming this way in a hurry.

Suddenly the bedroom door flew open and the captain strode in. He stopped short.

Daniel became a statue of himself: numb, unable to move, the incriminating document in his hand.

Sloper's look hardened. "What the hell are you doing in my room?"

Daniel swallowed.

"You know, I have a firing squad for people who steal my things."

His things? This didn't seem the moment to quibble.

"Maybe I should shoot you myself." He seemed to consider it seriously. "But why mess up the room? Anyway," he said, growing calmer as he spoke, "what's so fascinating about that sheet of parchment that you'd risk your life for it?"

"I didn't think I was risking my life."

"Oh, you didn't?"

"I didn't think you would kill an innocent person."

"So," he said, "the thief is innocent."

Daniel couldn't answer that.

"What about this map!" said Sloper, grabbing it from the boy's hands. "What is it? It has to be important."

Several plausible lies popped into the boy's head, but he wasn't able to say them.

"Well?"

"I don't really know."

"You're lying!"

The boy's initial panic had subsided, and he looked at the captain directly. "I wish I could, believe me."

Sloper assessed him through narrowed eyes. "All right," he said, "let's say you don't know what it is." He spread the map out and tapped it with his finger. "What do you *think* it is?"

"I think it's about the island."

"Island. What island? The one with the bird?" He bent

over the document. "So you think those are the other towns?"

"Maybe."

"And this in the middle . . ."

"Everwood, yes. Well, maybe."

"And what are these three little marks over here?"

"Symbols of some kind. I don't know."

"*I don't know,*" he mimicked. "You expect me to believe that?" His eyes narrowed again. "Apparently, you do."

The captain walked over to the window and stared into the darkness. "You sneak in here, risking your neck for a strange-looking map, and you tell me you don't know what it is! The crazy part of it is I believe you." He turned. "I'll tell you what I think. I think those marks are hiding places. I think the rebels have hidden caches of guns and ammunition."

"I'm sure you're wrong."

"Wrong, am I?" He examined the map again. "What else would it be? This whole town"—he waved his hand—"a nest of traitors!"

Part of Daniel was very frightened, but he was able to observe his fear, as if it were someone else's. The separation allowed him to think. His instincts told him Sloper was wrong about the map. But those markers. They had to be important, even sacred. Sacred symbols on an ancient map.

He remembered: The town was "protected."

Didn't feel like it now.

Even if Sloper was wrong, his mistake could lead him to find things his eyes weren't meant to see. Protections could be ripped away. Certainly, he wouldn't hesitate to destroy the town. He was planning to. He'd already killed a farmer.

"Think about it, sir. This map is very old."

"It's counterfeit! I see that now."

"No, it's much older than— What are you doing?"

Sloper had pulled out his own map of the region and was comparing coordinates. "I'm figuring out exactly where those guns are hidden!"

In a calm part of Daniel's mind, a place beneath the fear, he knew he couldn't let Sloper succeed. Better that *nobody* had the map.

"Let me bring the light over," Daniel said.

Sloper wasn't listening. He had a pencil out and was jotting down numbers.

"Here." The boy set the kerosene lamp on the desk and turned the toothed knob to bring up the wick and make the flame brighter.

Sloper grunted.

Daniel stood just outside the circle of light. He knew this might be the last minute of his life. *Can't be helped*, he thought. Picking up *The Arabian Nights*, a substantial volume, a special favorite, one that had taken him a whole week to read when he was younger, he suddenly smashed it against the lamp, shattering the glass shade and spilling flaming kerosene across the desk.

Even before Sloper could leap away, the map was burning.

D awn
Twelve

The room was an instant commotion of flame, kerosene stink, and howls of terrified rage.

Daniel, still clutching the book, was through the door and into the hallway by the time the lieutenant had started up the stairs, a coffee cup wobbling in his hands.

"Help!" Daniel shouted. "Fire in there!"

The soldier looked at him strangely before racing past.

Daniel caught a glimpse of the captain tearing a blanket off the bed and throwing it over the flames, all the while shouting at the soldier; but Daniel didn't hear what he said. In fact, he didn't remember getting downstairs. Only when the warm wind hit him did he realize he was outside dashing across the rutted ground to the barn. That's when he discovered he was holding a book—a book stinking of kerosene. Tossing it aside, he grabbed his bike and pushed it out to the road.

A glance back: no sign of flames—good—back door opening—bad—and a man running wildly out, a silhouette against the porch light. Daniel jumped on the bike. The man raised his arm as if pointing. There was a brief flash and a *thunk* as a bullet tore into the maple tree beside the boy's head. That was the end of thinking for a while. The bike skidded on loose dirt but righted itself as Daniel pedaled madly, the roadside bushes crowding him, whispering *Hurry!* as he rushed on through the dark.

What have I done?

Sweat blurred his vision, but he could make out something up ahead coming toward him. With his forearm he wiped his eyes.

A bicycle.

"Wes!"

The younger boy skidded to a stop. "Danny! What's going on?"

"Trouble. They're coming after me."

"What? Slow down. Who's after you?"

Daniel turned his head and saw a vague glimmer behind him, growing brighter. "Quick! Get off the road!"

"Danny . . ."

Daniel slid off his bike and pulled it into the bushes, his brother right behind him.

"Get down!" Daniel yelled in a whisper, just as the captain's staff car hove into view. It swerved past, spitting up dirt.

Cautiously the boys stood.

"Danny, what in the world . . . ?"

"I did something stupid."

"Kind of looks that way."

"We've got to find Emily."

The two of them started pedaling. Twice, as they approached the Byrdsong place, they had to veer into the bushes when cars roared by.

Finally, they abandoned their bikes in the underbrush and set out on foot through the trees. They made a wide circle around the house, keeping low, till they found the way. The underbrush grew thicker, but dawn was coming, vague light filtering through the foliage. The boys could see occasional broken twigs and scuff marks in the leaf mold.

"This way," Wesley whispered.

Daniel stopped. "There's no way Grandma Byrdsong could get through here."

"I know."

"Then what are we doing?"

"We're following Emily."

"Why would she . . . ?"

His brother was pushing ahead, not listening. Daniel followed.

The thorn trees grew more thickly as the boys got closer to the stream. Finally, they had to go on hands and knees, ignoring as best they could the pricks of brambles and the sharp-edged stones. From the bent thistle stalks, they could see that someone had come this way recently. Not far ahead, the stream was making quiet shuffling sounds, like an old man going through his papers.

A minute later, they broke through the last barrier of thorns. Mist, like a smoke screen, rose from the sluggish water.

"You all right?" Daniel whispered. "Your cheek is bleeding."

"You're not so pretty yourself."

They looked around. Bent grasses.

"Emily?" whispered Wesley.

No answer. They followed the stream.

Thirty feet ahead they saw a dark bundle at the edge of the water. It was Emily, sitting with her legs drawn up.

"Hey," said Daniel softly.

She didn't look at him. In her lap, mewing piteously, was a white cat.

Daniel crouched. Wes stood a few feet back.

"That's her favorite, isn't it?" Daniel said. "The one called Mallow?"

She turned toward him and nodded, shaking loose a tear from her brimming eyes. "And look." She pointed to a deep indentation at the water's brink. A small, square hole. Daniel remembered Bridey's sturdy, square-heeled shoes.

He looked across the stream. V-shaped ripples slid slowly by, revealing a horrible-headed snake. It continued on past, its body a waving shadow beneath the surface.

Part Two
HERE

Freckles

Thirteen

The three friends started back. They'd been up all night and were exhausted. It was especially hard going for Emily, who refused to have anyone else carry the cat. The creature was somehow a part of her grandmother, maybe all there was left, and she wasn't going to let go of it.

"Hey," she called out.

Daniel turned.

"Did we just go through some poison ivy or something? My shoulder's itching really fierce."

"Poison ivy, poison oak, lots of stuff. But you've got long sleeves."

"It feels like my shoulder's burning up."

"Let's get you to the cave," said Daniel. "We've got that first-aid kit."

"Why not the house?"

He shook his head. "Later."

They struggled on. The cat was the only one comfortable, secure in the crook of Emily's arm. Gradually thorn trees were replaced by oaks and beeches, and thistles gave way to rocks and moss. Sunlight was now hitting the tops of the taller trees and beginning to shinny down the trunks, turning the woods golden.

"This way," said Daniel, cutting east.

They continued in silence. Daniel saw Emily wince, but she didn't say anything. At last, they reached the hill leading up to the cave.

"Is it bad?" he said.

"Let's just get up there."

They started climbing, Wes leading the way, his brother bringing up the rear. They were relieved to see that the campsite hadn't been disturbed.

"This is supposed to help with itches," said Daniel, unscrewing a tube of white ointment from the medicine kit. "Let's take a look."

She hesitated, but then set the cat down and turned away and undid the top few buttons. Daniel pulled the material away from her shoulders.

He paused.

"Aren't you going to put it on?" she said.

"Um, this is not poison ivy. And it's not thorns."

"Definitely not thorns," said Wesley.

"Does everybody have to look at me?" said Emily, blushing.

"Seems to me," said Daniel with a smile, "you've got a bad case of freckles."

"I do *not* have freckles!" protested Emily. "I've never had freckles."

"Well, you have them now."

"Freckles don't burn."

"Wait." He examined her shoulder blades closely. Something about the pattern struck him as familiar, the spray of brownish dots swirling like a constellation across her back from one shoulder to the other.

"What?" she said, irritated. She wasn't used to having a boy—two boys!—staring at her bare skin.

"Emily," he said quietly. "You're not going to believe this, but these freckles look an awful lot like that map of yours."

"What?" She pulled the top of her dress tight and buttoned it. "Don't be ridiculous."

"It *does* look like the map. Only . . . different."

"Only different."

"Let me look again."

"No!"

"It looks like the map, only changed around somehow."

"Daniel Crowley—"

"I wish I had a mirror. I could show you."

"I can't believe you're being so crazy. God! I just lost my grandmother!"

"I know." Actually, he hadn't been able to believe that Bridey might be dead. His mind had put that possibility aside.

"And this," Emily went on angrily, looking back at her shoulder, "whatever it is—is burning like crazy!"

"Sorry. Look. Let me put the stuff on."

"No more crazy talk!"

"I promise." Daniel and Wesley looked at each other.

Grudgingly Emily undid the buttons again, and Daniel carefully smeared on the ointment. "Better?"

She expelled an irritated little sigh. "Maybe." The cat

was sniffing at the stones around the fire pit. "Now," she said, pulling the cat onto her lap, "anyone want to tell me why we didn't just go to the house?"

Wes looked at his brother. "You'd better tell her. Actually, I'm not too clear on it, either."

Daniel sat on a stone and leaned his elbows on his knees, clasping his hands. "Captain Sloper . . . ," he began, and paused. "I got him pretty mad at me."

"I thought you were his teacher's pet," she said, rather meanly. "Telling him everybody's secrets."

"Dan's not kidding!" said Wes. "You should've seen those soldiers running around trying to find him."

"What did you do?" she said tightly.

Daniel rubbed his forehead. "Okay. Here's the thing."

He told the story as simply as possible, making no excuses. Excuses would have felt like lies, and his nervous system wouldn't have put up with that. When he finished, even the cat was still.

"So," she said slowly, "you got a madman trying to kill you, *and* you burned up the map."

"It wasn't his fault," said Wesley.

"Who cares whose fault it is? How are we supposed to get to the island?"

Another silence, this one broken by the cat's weak meow. It probably hadn't eaten since yesterday.

"Emily," said Daniel, "we may have a map after all."

"Don't start about that."

"If we could only get a mirror so you could see . . ."

"Why do you keep doing this?"

"You don't believe me."

"Of course not."

"But, Emily, don't you see? I'm the only person you can *always* believe."

She looked down at the cat. The cat looked up at her and mewed.

"We've got to feed this thing."

Daniel watched her.

"We'll take her back to Grandma's house," she said. "I'll go in by myself." She looked at the brothers. "While I'm at it, I suppose I can take a look in a mirror."

"Great!" said Daniel.

"And can you bring back some paper and a pencil?" Daniel's kid brother was always practical.

"What for?"

"We might need to copy down your freckles."

She looked at him and shook her head. "You're as crazy as your brother."

Wesley smiled. He didn't at all mind being called crazy.

Emily breezed into the house through the big front door to find four soldiers in the parlor talking in low tones.

"Hello, everybody," she said.

Only one of the soldiers looked up.

"I found Mallow in the woods," said the girl.

No one was paying attention.

"Had any luck?" she asked.

"Luck doing what?" said one.

"Finding my grandmother."

"Not yet."

Emily frowned. They weren't looking for her grandmother. They weren't *thinking* of looking for her grandmother. After last night's flurry of concern, they'd moved on to other things.

She went past into the kitchen and got out the dry cat food for Mallow. The poor creature did figure eights around her ankles and cried loudly as Emily filled the dish.

"There you go." She stood back and watched the cat attack the food, closing its eyes in concentration as it crunched loudly. Soon other cats appeared, a big gray and an orange-and-black tabby with a white nose.

Emily set out a bowl of fresh water, then grabbed a banana for herself and hurried upstairs. Sunlight poured in through the spring window. Why hadn't she just left the map there, where it was safe?

She looked around. On the night table lay a yellow pad and a couple of pencils. She slipped them into her crocheted shoulder bag. Then she touched the photograph of her mother for luck, as she always did when she went out, and headed down the stairs.

"Now, where do you think you're going?"

A large-bellied sergeant named Dominick blocked the door as Emily was hurrying across the front hall. With his bulbous forehead and cheeks disfigured by smallpox, he was the one soldier Emily always tried to avoid.

"Nowhere."

"You going to see that Crowley kid? We're looking for him."

"Why would I want to see him?"

"What's in the bag?"

"Nothing."

"Let's see." He reached a ham-sized hand inside and pulled out the pad.

"I like to draw."

The man frowned. "Draw what?"

"Flowers? Trees? Bunnies?"

He handed the pad back and Emily went to the door, stopping in front of the backwards mirror. She glanced at Dominick, but he'd already turned away. Quickly she undid a few buttons of her dress and pulled the material aside. Her back's reflection was right in front of her, and across it lay a weirdly familiar pattern, written in freckles. She stared. Noticing a soldier glancing her way, she buttoned up and ducked out the door, her heart beating with a strange excitement.

She found the boys where she'd left them, behind a bushy hemlock just inside the lip of the woods.

"How's the shoulder feel?" said Daniel.

"Hadn't noticed."

They moved deeper into the woods and cut over to the cave. Emily sat down on her favorite rock. "All right," she admitted, "they do look like freckles. I don't get it."

"Do they look like the map?" said Wesley, who'd never seen the map himself.

"Maybe. Kind of." She turned to Daniel. "You burn the map," she murmured, "so the map is burned into *me*?"

"Did you bring some paper?" said Wesley. "We'd better copy this down."

"Do you mind?" said Daniel.

"Go ahead."

Of the three of them, Wesley was the best sketcher, and so he did the drawing while Emily tried to hold still.

"Don't wiggle!" said Wesley, erasing several dots.

"I got an itch!"

"I can't do this if you keep moving."

Emily cast a sidelong glance at Daniel.

The result wasn't perfect, but close enough. The question was how to use it. Daniel squinted at three little marks on three sides of a larger blotch (the island?) and thought about the original document. He turned to Wesley. "In your geography class, you studied maps, right?"

"We're doing a whole unit on them."

"What do you make of this one?"

Wesley frowned. "Without any place names or longitude or latitude?"

True, there were no place names, but Daniel remembered little spiral symbols on three sides of the central area—like seashells twisting three turns to the left. He described them.

"I remember that," said Emily. "I'd forgotten they curved to the left."

"Counterclockwise."

"Lefty loosey," she murmured.

"What?" said Daniel.

"Righty tighty, lefty loosey. That's what Grandma taught me about opening jars."

"I wish she'd said something about opening the island."

"What are you *talking* about?" Wesley demanded.

They looked at the map again.

"Do you remember the words around the edge?" said

Daniel. "I couldn't make them out. Something about a serpent?"

"I think I figured it out," said Emily. "It said, 'Cover the Serpent with Next Spring's Earth.'" She looked around at the others.

"That's it?" said Wesley.

"There's a little more. It doesn't make sense, either. 'Three times Round for the Heart's Rebirth.'"

"You're right," he said. "It's senseless."

"Cover the serpent," Daniel murmured.

"Maybe," she said, "we should go back to that spiral. You say it goes three times to the left?"

Wesley stood up. "Wait a minute. Is it anything like that mark in the back of the cave?"

The other two looked at him blankly.

"I'll show you. Give me the flashlight."

The three of them crowded through the narrow opening. The flashlight cast strange shadows, but there along the back wall, among initials and chalked dates (some going back twenty years), was a deeply etched spiral, not an easy thing to inscribe in such hard rock. It curved three times to the left.

"That's it!" Daniel cried.

Emily's eyes shone.

"Do you think," she said as they stumbled outside, "this is one of the places on the map?"

"One of three points," suggested Daniel, pointing to strategic freckle-shaped marks on three sides of the island.

Wesley looked him doubtfully. "Pretty far-fetched."

"The scientist speaks," said Daniel dryly.

Emily tossed her curls. "But where are the other two? And," she said slowly, "do you think the spiral could possibly be a serpent?"

They looked at one another.

Emily's mouth edged into a smile.

 The S*piral* *Fourteen*

Wesley was the kind of kid who needed to do things right. "Before we go smearing dirt around in the cave," he said, "let me get my county map. It's a lot more exact than this thing." He looked at the crude drawing he'd made.

Daniel nodded.

"But hurry back," said Emily.

So Wesley went up to the house for his map, protractor, compass, and, to be on the safe side, a pocketful of brownies his mother had made.

While there, he told her about Daniel, that he was okay but wouldn't be back for dinner or anything else until things cooled down with Sloper.

Gwen Crowley was alarmed. She'd been alarmed since last night, when she came home to find the house stinking of smoke and Daniel's room ruined. She paced around the kitchen clasping and unclasping her hands and wouldn't sit down. She'd talk to the captain, she said, when he came in and get him to promise not to hurt her son.

"Emily says not to trust him, no matter what he promises."

"Oh, I don't. Where's Danny? Is he at the cave?"

"Uh-huh."

"Are you coming back, at least?"

"I don't know. Actually, we're trying to get onto the island."

"Wesley, no! Do you know how dangerous that is?"

"I know, Mom, but we think we've found a map."

"Who is we? You and Daniel?"

"And Emily."

"Emily's with you? Wait." She took out a bag and filled it with ham slices, crusty bread, a hunk of yellow cheese, and a bag of pine nuts. For good measure, she tossed in a couple of apples. "Here, it's all I can spare, but it should keep you fed for a little while."

Wes wedged it into his backpack.

"Just a minute," said Gwen. "Get your brother's canteen."

She filled it with cold water from the pump.

"Thanks, Mom."

"You be careful, now," she said, watching as he hurried off, jumping down the two stone steps, then cutting across the Fishes' backyard and heading for the woods.

She watched long after he was out of sight.

The two friends sat together on the boulder above the cave. The sun beat down on them with a special emphasis.

"Spring earth," Emily murmured, turning the drawing over in her hands.

Daniel shook his head. "No, *next* spring's earth."

"And here we are in the middle of summer. Wait a minute!" She sat up straight. Then she stood up. "Yes."

"Yes, what?"

She looked at him excitedly. "Stay here and wait for Wesley."

"Where are you going?"

"To Grandma's house. Don't worry. I'll be quick."

"Em . . ."

But she'd already climbed down and was scampering off through the woods.

Yes, she thought. *Of course!*

By the time she reached the house, she was sweating. "Forget something?" Big Dominick watched Emily hurry past, through the hall and up the staircase.

Breathless, she reached the top floor and burst into her room. She paused, trying to remember which was the spring window. As she cranked open the nearest one, several dry leaves blew in on a chilly breeze.

The next window gave her a view of budding trees swaying in gentle sunlight. Part of the garden was visible, and the earth looked freshly turned. *Good,* she thought, but was she seeing last spring or next spring? *Just have to take my chances.* A trellis thick with greening ivy covered the whole side of the house. Would it hold her? It was a long way to the ground.

With her hand, she tested one of the wooden slats and found it springy, even flimsy; but the ivy's roots gripped the wall firmly. It occurred to her that this might not be the smartest idea she'd ever had.

She tried to think of some other way. There was none. Taking a deep breath, she swung a leg over and started down.

The two brothers looked up with relief to see Emily stagger-ing toward them carrying a pail filled with dirt. Daniel ran to help her.

"We were worried you weren't coming back."

"Almost didn't," she said, catching her breath. "Ever try climbing up a wall while lugging a pail of dirt?"

Daniel smiled. "I don't think so."

"Well, don't."

"Here, take a drink of water. Wesley brought a canteen from the house."

She nodded thanks and took a deep drink, ending with a gasp.

"You want to tell us what this is about?" said Daniel.

She sat down by the extinct fire pit. It seemed she was trying not to smile. "Feast your eyes," she said, "on next spring's earth."

Eagerly, she told about her adventure and the strange feeling it gave her to enter a different season—and to bring a bucketful of the future back to the present.

"Now," said Wesley, "all we have to do is figure out where to put that wonderful dirt."

"Well, we think we know one place," she said.

"Yeah, but there have to be others."

Wesley spread out the county map he'd brought from the house. Beside it he laid the map he'd drawn. He was good at this kind of thing—math, geometry, geography, anything to do with calculations. Daniel let him work.

While they waited, Emily and Daniel looked into making sandwiches. "Here," Emily said, handing a ham sandwich and a brownie to Wesley. "Brain food."

The boy took absentminded bites as he refigured his work. "The original map was very old, right? Rock formations might be the only things left. This cave, for instance."

"So," said Emily, "we need to find two other formations?"

"I know where they *should* be," said Wesley, shouldering his backpack. "Let's see if they're there."

"And we're supposed to go counterclockwise," said Daniel.

"Three times around?" said Emily.

Daniel held up his hand. "First, let's do this one."

They went in the back of the cave, Emily holding the flashlight. She reached into the pail for some dirt, but found it wouldn't stay in the groove of the spiral. Daniel dribbled in some water from the canteen, making mud, and she had better luck with that. In fact, the design was soon covered, leaving only a dark patch on the wall.

She stood back, admiring her messy work. "Now for the other two."

With the help of Wesley's compass and the county map, it wasn't long before they found a likely formation. It was a single vertical boulder rising like a monolith from the hillside. They walked around it slowly, looking for markings. They didn't find any.

"I wonder," said Wesley. He knelt and started scooping dirt away from the base. "This is on a hill. Over the years, the soil would have built up on the back side."

A foot below the surface, there it was. Emily traced the

spiral gently with her finger. She looked up at the boys and smiled brightly.

"One more to go," said Wesley.

Finding it was easier said than done—the brambles treacherous, the branches fiercely resistant. At last they came to a cavelike structure formed of several boulders thrown together. And there, on the side of the largest rock, half-hidden under ivy, was the third spiral. The kids jumped around, shouting and laughing.

"We did it!" Wesley cried.

"Miss Byrdsong," said Daniel grandly. "If you please!"

She gave a little bow and dug her hand into the muck.

After she'd covered the spiral, the friends continued around the perimeter of the island, crossing bridges where necessary, till they arrived back where they'd started.

"Now," said Daniel, giving the cave's boulder a pat, "two more times."

Emily nodded, her face flushed.

"Are we supposed to put on more dirt?" said Wesley.

"I hope not," Emily said. "We just used up the last of it."

"Let's go around again and see what happens," said Daniel.

Along the way, they noticed that the woods looked different—thicker, wilder than it had a few minutes before. By the time they reached the final set of boulders, they almost didn't recognize the place, it was so grown over. A badger skittered out from the opening in the rocks and waddled away.

They continued on, breathing hard, until they made it back to the campsite.

"Ready for the last circle?" said Daniel.

Emily was leaning against the side of the cave, catching her breath. "Hey," she said, looking around. "Where is everything?"

Wesley had a panicked look. "Where's my stuff? Did somebody take it?"

Daniel stared at the place where the fire pit had been. The ground was thickly covered in scrub bushes. "We must be at the wrong cave," he said.

Wesley shook his head. "Look at the rocks. Same slant, same shape."

"I'll check in the back," said Daniel, heading inside. He came out seconds later, preceded by a burst of frightened bats. "The spiral's still there. Still covered with mud. But nothing else."

"What about our supplies?" said Wesley.

"Gone!"

"Okay," said Emily, "I know I'm not crazy."

Daniel rubbed his chin. "It's like each turn around the island takes us to some other place."

Emily looked down. "No," she said slowly. "Not some other place. Some other time."

"That's dumb," said Wes.

"You think so? It's like the windows in my room. The spring window, say. You turn one handle, you see next spring. Turn the other one, you see last spring."

Wesley raised an eyebrow.

"Where do you think I got the spring earth?"

"I don't know," said Wesley. "All I know is somebody stole my things."

"Maybe they don't exist back here."

"Back where?"

She looked at him as though he were thick.

"Look," he said. "I don't believe in this stuff. It's just a bunch of superstition."

Emily checked the urge to fire back. She remembered saying the same thing to her grandmother. "Well," she said, "we've got one more turn around the island. Why don't we see what happens?"

This time the woods grew even wilder, practically impassable, no sign of a path. Overhead, grapevines draped the closely set trees. Emily gasped when a brace of pheasants exploded out from under a holly tree.

They almost passed the marker without seeing it, so thickly covered it was with vinca and Virginia creeper. Wesley just stood and stared.

Daniel came up beside him. "This must be the way it looked long ago."

"I don't believe that," said Wes.

The third marker, three massive boulders, looked the most different of all. The rocks were no longer leaning against each other, but standing upright, their back ends wedged securely in the hillside. Suddenly Emily grabbed Daniel's arm as a silver fox trotted out of the shadows, its shiny coat catching the sunlight. The creature stopped to look at the humans, as if they were only mildly interesting, then disappeared into a thicket.

"I've never seen one of those before," Wes breathed.

Daniel agreed. "Not around here. They were hunted to extinction before Grandpa's time."

They continued on. Rounding the far side of the island, they broke free of the trees. To their amazement, the thistles, firethorn, and poison oak that had barred their way had mostly disappeared. In their place stood swaying, waist-high flowers, a tide of white and rose mallow blooms such as they had never seen.

"This looks like an easy way to get to the stream," Daniel said.

"Why didn't we know about this?" said Wes.

They waded through the flowers as through waves of applause, and soon found themselves at the stream bank.

"Hey," said Wesley. "What happened?"

Where wide, murky water had made its surly way around an unreachable island, there was now nothing more than a brook, clear and bright in the late sunlight, and so narrow it could easily be jumped across.

"Impossible," said Wesley under his breath.

Emily looked at him, remembering. "That's what Grandma Byrdsong said. It's an impossible island."

"Actually," said Daniel, "right now it looks *very* possible."

She nodded. "It kind of does."

"So," he said, looking at the others. "Who wants to go first?"

The H*iding* Place
Fifteen

"Your son," said Sloper as the men prepared to sit down to dinner. "Quite a boy."

"You mean Daniel?" said Crowley, taking his seat.

Three of Sloper's aides pulled out their straight-backed chairs and sat down heavily.

"He risked a great deal last night to steal the map from me."

"Map?"

"Please, my friend, don't insult me by pretending you don't know."

"Where *is* Daniel?" Crowley glanced around as if he might have overlooked him. "And Wesley." He turned to his wife, just then coming in with the roast chicken—a skinny one. It had been the last bird left in the coop. "Gwen? Have you seen the boys?"

She shook her head. "If you mean Danny, not since last night." She set the platter on hot pads and stepped back. "When we were all out there searching for Bridey."

"He didn't come back?" said her husband.

"Ever since the boys started sleeping in the barn, I hardly know *where* they are."

"They didn't show up at the store, either."

"Enough," interrupted the captain, bunching his napkin in his fist. "You can stop the charade. I know what you're up to." He looked around the table. "Don't look surprised."

Crowley's face was a nest of confusion. "Captain," he said, "you have to forgive me. My children don't tell me what they're doing. What were you saying about a map?"

Sloper briefly closed his eyes. "Don't."

"But . . ."

"Next you'll tell me you don't know about the caches of weapons hidden in the woods."

"Weapons?"

"It was all there on the map." Sloper leaned back in his chair. "*As you very well know.*"

"As I . . . ?"

Sloper held up a hand. "Please. You lie so badly."

"Gwen," said Crowley, "do you know about this?"

Mrs. Crowley lifted her head bravely. "Just that there was a fire upstairs in Daniel's room."

"Well, we all know that," said her husband. "You can smell it all over the house."

Gwen turned to the captain. "How is it up there now? Is it livable? I've been airing it out all afternoon."

Sloper slammed his fist down on the table. Wine sloshed from the glasses and the chicken jumped on the platter. "*Damn it!* Stop!"

No one spoke.

"We know," Sloper growled, "that three children are missing: your two boys and that girl over at the Byrdsong place. We also know that your boy was willing to burn down the house to keep me from reading the map."

Crowley opened his mouth to speak, but thought better of it.

"Why?" Sloper's eyes narrowed. "Why would he do a thing like that?"

Again, Crowley almost spoke.

"I'll tell you why," the captain supplied. He refilled his wine glass and drained it in a gulp. "He was afraid I'd learn the secret. But we all know the secret, don't we? We know the weapons are stored on the island!"

"What!"

"So simple," the captain continued. "So clever. Who would think this quaint backwater town was a hotbed of insurrection? Very likely it's the supply post for the whole rebellion!"

"Now that's ridic—"

"An island no one can get to. A place everyone's afraid of, surrounded by superstition, protected by quicksand and snakes."

"Captain, listen," Crowley objected.

"If I wanted to hide something, I couldn't find a better place. But since your son has deprived us of the map, we don't know the precise locations. So we'll just have to shell the whole island."

Gwen stood up, her hand fluttering to her chest. "You wouldn't."

"You know we're planning to test out our new artillery,"

said Sloper. "Let's see if we can't blow up some weapons at the same time—along with anybody who happens to be over there guarding them."

Gwen's face froze.

Sloper looked up at her. The ghost of a smile played around the corners of his mouth. "What is it, Mrs. Crowley? You don't look well."

An I Impossible Island

The island was edged with evergreens and curtained with vines. Stepping through them was like leaving the sunny out-doors and entering a cathedral, with ceilings so high they were lost in the gloom. Once within, the three friends found that the evergreens tapered off quickly. Beyond lay an open woods of massive trees. Daniel thought he knew every kind of tree there was, but many of these he didn't recognize.

There was a scent in the air, too, familiar yet elusive, and the sounds, half-lost in the foliage, of many birds, whole choirs of them, singing and hushed at the same time.

Wesley, always the scientist, bent down to examine the dark-leaved bushes he was wading through. It was then that he saw the violets beneath. The forest was carpeted with them, the air giddy with perfume.

They walked on, marveling at how much taller these trees were than the ones they knew. These woods had never been thinned by loggers or tamed by campers. Muscular vines climbed huge trunks and disappeared in the forest canopy.

Daniel suddenly froze as he realized that one of those vines, thicker than the others, was not a vine at all. Large as a fire hose, a gleaming green snake was making its way slowly up over the chunky bark of a chestnut oak.

Wes saw it, too. Then Emily. No one said anything. Probably no one breathed.

They went on. They went on for quite a while.

"Did you see *that?*" said Emily suddenly.

The boys looked where she was pointing. A flash of red and a moment of black that could have been anything. Then the foliage grew still.

Daniel didn't know whether to investigate or keep on the way they were going. They decided to keep going.

"Hey, Danny," said Wes after a while. He stopped to catch his breath. "Shouldn't we be getting to the other side?" He ran his arm across his forehead.

"You'd think," said Emily.

They pushed on another ten minutes. Daniel would have been happy to keep going. Just breathing the scented air gave him a feeling of lightness, as if gravity were somehow less grave here, and his pack lighter. But his brother was worn out.

"Wait," Wesley called out. "I gotta sit down."

They found a fallen tree, like a giant's outflung arm, and sat on its wrist.

"Sure this isn't a snake?" said Emily, smiling.

"Drink of water?" Daniel offered. They all took sips from the canteen. He looked at his brother. "You okay?"

"In case you don't remember, we didn't get any sleep last night. And we've been hiking all day."

"I know. The place looks a lot bigger from the inside than from the outside."

"It's like it doesn't end."

"Are you all right to keep going?"

Wesley shrugged.

Daniel nodded. "You too, Em?"

She lifted her head, listening. "Wait." She held up a hand. "What's that?"

A distant sound, almost like a woman's voice, hovered in the air, sourceless. Then a breeze picked up, rustling through laurel and rhododendron, and for some seconds they couldn't hear anything else.

The breeze subsided. There it was again, distant but unmistakable, a woman's voice. It was singing!

"Mama!" cried Emily. She set off at a run.

"Wait for us!" Daniel started after her.

Wesley tried to keep up, but he was really tired. The girl was already out of sight and his brother nearly so.

Daniel glanced back. He *had* to catch up with Emily, but there was his brother, struggling. "Hey," he called, "come on!"

"I'm coming!" He wasn't coming very fast, though.

"She's too far ahead! We'll lose her!"

"You go on." He was leaning against a tree.

Daniel started back. "Hey, kid," he said. The brothers sat down at the foot of a juniper. The ground just there was covered with moss, green, soft, and damp. "You okay?"

Wes nodded.

"Just winded?"

No answer.

"Let's see that backpack," said Daniel. "Anything left to eat?"

"Sure." The boy rummaged through and came up with bread, cheese, an apple, and half a brownie. The pine nuts had spilled into the bottom of the pack, among the lint and crumbs. Saving some food for Emily, he put together a sandwich and cut it in half.

The brothers sat cross-legged, not speaking. The wind had died away where they were, but high above them, in the leafy canopy, it was making a racket. Underneath that sound was another, low-pitched and steady—not a human voice this time, but as if the world were humming to itself.

"Strange place," said Wesley, yawning.

"It is."

They fell silent, hoping to hear Emily trudging back toward them, but she didn't appear. There was only the wash of wind, the scuttle of squirrels, and the thousand barely audible sounds of an intense but invisible life.

Wes got comfortable on a cushion of moss and leaves. The scent of violets drifted over him.

"Tell you what," said Daniel. "Why don't you rest while I try to find Emily?" He pulled a red bandanna from his pocket and tied it to an overhead branch. "This'll help me find you."

His brother answered with a grunt, already half-asleep.

Good old Wes, thought Daniel. *He's had a tough day.* He turned and headed in the direction Emily had taken, looking for scuffed leaves and the occasional snapped twig that would tell him where she'd gone.

He thought he heard something—something beyond the noises he was making. Stopping to look around, he saw a tall linden tree some thirty feet distant, its top swaying unnaturally. There was that flash of color again, a patch of red within the dark green of the foliage. Daniel squinted and for a brief moment saw clearly: a man, small and wiry, wearing an old-fashioned red waistcoat.

"Hey!" Daniel hurried toward him, but the man was gone. "Who are you?"

Nothing.

How can there be somebody on an island no one can get to?

Well, he would find Emily, at least. But there were no signs to go by, no singing voice to follow. The light, dim to begin with, was growing vaguer as afternoon declined toward evening. The woods were crowded with shadows. He was up to his waist in them. Then up to his neck. He continued on, but with the sun going, and then gone, it was hard to judge his direction. Another ten minutes and he had to admit it: he was lost.

"Wes!" he called out. "Emily!"

He listened hard, but could hear only the whispered confidences of leaves and the occasional snap of a twig as night animals began to stir. Alone in the forest, he felt surrounded, hemmed in. To shake the feeling, he ran on, heedless now of his direction. He tripped over a fallen branch and went sprawling, scraping his forearm where he'd tried to break his fall.

Now that was smart!

Still on hands and knees, he looked up, and the breath suddenly caught in his throat, for he found himself staring at something not to be believed: a ghostly leopard, milk white, not twenty feet away, sitting in profile like a sphinx under the boughs of a juniper tree. Amazed, he watched as the great cat slowly turned its head to look at him, its eyes clear blue and impersonal as ice.

Daniel hardly breathed, lest the apparition vanish, or worse, pounce and tear him to pieces. He was sure there could be no defense against those bright, in-curving fangs.

Silently the leopard rose to its feet. It walked off a short distance, stopped, and looked back.

Go on! I'm too scrawny for you to eat!

The animal went a few steps farther, then stopped again, looking back.

What do you want? Then the answer came. *He wants me to follow him!*

"I don't think so," Daniel said aloud.

The animal tilted its head quizzically. Then it turned, walked a few more steps, and looked back.

The boy started to follow, keeping his distance and trying not to make noise in the ankle-deep leaves. The creature trotted ahead and again stopped.

Daniel's fear was great, but he went on, his heart beating hard.

Evening, meanwhile, had perfected itself into night. Small, nameless creatures scuttled through nearby bushes, and a screech owl let out a scream from the fortress of an oak. Daniel hardly noticed. He was concentrating on the retreating whiteness ahead of him. Always beyond reach, it never disappeared entirely.

Then it did, just as Daniel stumbled free of the underbrush to find himself in a clearing amid tall grasses silvered with moonlight. Nor was moonlight the only illumination. A glimmer of phosphorescent moss lit the grasses from beneath, giving the place an unearthly glow.

Daniel searched the surrounding darkness, but the creature that had led him here was nowhere in sight. Had he seen what he thought he'd seen?

Creatures like that don't exist! he told himself. *Not in this part of the world.*

The wind gusted up, turning the grasses into silver-tipped waves. That's when he heard the humming, low and soft, and realized it was coming from the surrounding trees. In that part of the forest, the trees were tall and thin, like tuning forks, and Daniel guessed the wind blowing through them had created the strange, almost human sound.

He started across. The thigh-high grasses were flinging about in the wind, and he was struck by the wild beauty of the scene. Then, abruptly, he stopped, fear spiking as he realized how close he'd come to walking straight into an immense spider web, some ten feet across. It was only because of the moonlight that he'd seen it, the myriad strands transmuted into spun silver.

Gradually the panic subsided. There was no sign of the creature that had spun the web, connecting it to trees on either side of the clearing, but it was bound to be nearby. He could only imagine its size.

As a breeze made the web shimmer, something about it caught his eye. He realized there was a pattern within the pattern, and that at the center of the web's great spiral stood an upright rectangle, several feet tall, outlined not in pale silver but in white gold, or golden white, like moonlight laced with sunlight.

A *door*, he thought. He remembered the stories he'd heard from the old farmers when they'd come into his dad's grocery store. They'd talked about a mysterious door in the forest that led—well, they didn't know where it led. How could they? It was just a story they'd heard as children.

Daniel didn't remember their saying anything about a leopard, much less why it should lead him to this strange place. That was for him to discover.

He dared not think the next thought, but the thought came anyway: *It's a door. I'm supposed to go through it.*

What, he wondered, if it were a trap? What if the island were evil, as some thought? What if he were being lured to a horrible death? After all, to be caught in a web and . . . and *eaten*!

In spite of the warmth of the night, he found himself shivering. He wanted fiercely to turn back. And he should. Wesley needed him. His little brother shouldn't be left alone out there in the forest.

But Daniel knew he was making excuses. What he feared stood right in front of him, trembling.

A door.

I'm supposed to go through it.

He could tell himself it was for Emily, to find and rescue her. He could say it was for Bridey Byrdsong, that strangely lovable witch-woman who had so thoroughly disappeared. But the truth, at that final, fateful moment, was that he just *had* to know what was on the other side.

He held out his arm before him, took a deep shuddering breath, and stepped forward.

Seventeen
Wesley's Dream

Wes Crowley dreamed that he was dreaming.

In the rustling darkness, he saw glowing eyes: split yellow eyes, heartless blue eyes, infernal red eyes, coming closer, closer still. But he refused to listen to his fear. *It's all right*, he told himself. *I'm just dreaming.*

Then Wes Crowley dreamed that he woke up.

He raised his head from the varnished floor in the back corner of the classroom. He didn't know why he was lying there when his desk was up front, and the teacher, that nice Miss Temple, was calling on him.

"Sorry," he heard himself say as he hurried past snickering classmates to his seat.

Her hand was on her hip. "Wesley, did you hear a word I said?"

He shook his head. "No, ma'am."

"I want you to look at the blackboard."

He did, but nothing was written there.

"What does it say, Wesley? Tell the class."

This time, six words appeared. "This number," he read out loud, "is not a number." He looked at his teacher. "But there *isn't* any number."

"That's why it is not a number."

"But . . ."

He could see that Miss Temple, nice as she was, and pretty besides, was getting impatient. "Why won't you read what it says?"

The other kids were giggling. Their laughter turned into the twittering of birds.

He squinted. The words wouldn't stay still. "This sentence," he read, "cannot be read."

Bird songs filled the air.

"Wesley, pay attention!"

He tried again. "A bird," he read, concentrating hard, "is not a bird."

"That's impossible!"

"The island is not an island."

"Impossible!"

"A lie is not a lie."

"Wesley, leave the classroom!"

"But I checked my math!" Close to tears, he stood up. "I checked it!"

He bolted into the hall and outside to the deserted playing field, his eyes blurring. As he ran, he glanced at the darkening sky. *A bird is not a cloud,* he thought distractedly. *A cloud is not a cat.*

He hadn't watched where he was going and ran right into

a large man, solid as a wall. A soldier, he realized. Then he recognized the bulbous forehead and pox-riddled cheeks of the person grinning down at him.

"The captain's been looking for you."

Wes shook his head, denying all, struggling to twist free of the man's inhuman grip.

"He wants to bury you in a corner of the field."

"No!"

"He says not to worry. He says your death is not your death."

Suddenly Wesley's eyes flew open.

Inches from his face, staring at him with ice blue eyes, was a white leopard.

The B Eighteen lue Pavilion

As soon as his face had touched the web, Daniel had involuntarily shut his eyes, and now that he'd gotten through and was on the other side, he found them hard to open. A sticky mist had sealed the lids, cooled his face, and soaked his clothes.

At least he had gotten through!

Disgusting, he thought, wiping a wet hand across his face. With his fingers, he pried the lids open.

What he saw amazed him. Instead of darkness, a brightening dawn rose up just ahead, with sunlight turning the grasses tawny and glinting off a dome of some kind, light blue, rising through the distant canopy.

He turned and looked behind him. There lay night, darker by contrast than before, and the web he'd just stepped through. He saw the ragged tear he'd made, and behind it the black outline of trees. He watched, transfixed, as a shadow encroached on the web's upper corner. Slowly it crept downward toward the torn section. It was the spider, monstrous, its numerous legs stepping delicately from strand to glistening strand, like hairy fingers plucking the strings of a harp.

Daniel couldn't look away.

The creature, an obscene, round-bellied silhouette, passed across the opening where the door had been, then turned, crossed again, and turned again, each crossing leaving a taut new strand behind it.

The beast was sewing the door shut!

Within a few seconds, you couldn't see where the hole had ever been. The monster rested beside it awhile, then slowly climbed to its lurking place in an upper corner.

There would be no way back for Daniel. Not the way he'd come.

Shaken, he turned and started toward the blue dome he'd glimpsed before. As he came closer, it showed itself in its full grandeur: brilliant as a palace, simple as a hut, many-faceted, bigger than any house Daniel had ever seen, including Bridey's. It was so bright it made him wince to look at it straight on. He approached, afraid but in control of his fear. He would knock on the door, he decided, and deal with whatever happened.

The problem was, he couldn't find a door to knock on. The dome appeared seamless. He walked around it slowly, peering in the translucent panels, but couldn't make anything out. Hesitantly he reached out a hand to see what the facets felt like. That gave him the greatest surprise of all. Touching the curved surface was like touching a cloud. A portion of the wall, which had looked so solid, swirled aside like blue mist disturbed by an air current.

He stepped through. The wall reconstituted itself behind him, and he found himself inside a grand pavilion, blue floor, blue wall, blue air, all glowing in morning light.

That's when he noticed, across the room, an elegant divan in the eighteenth-century style. On it sat a woman and a girl in deep conversation. *This is a dream*, he thought, even as they turned to look at him.

"Emily!" He ran over, filled with joyous disbelief.

The girl smiled. "Hello, Daniel."

The woman beside her rose to her feet. She was tall, Daniel realized, taller than he was, with large, gentle eyes and delicate features. She reminded him, somehow, of a tumbling stream, from her long, loose curls, set off by a sprig of violets, to the flowing dress that might have been white except for the pervasive blueness of the air.

"Well," she said, lifting her chin, "Daniel Crowley. I understand you're the one who burned the map."

He flushed. "I'm sorry, I didn't mean . . ."

She stopped him with her smile. It was a smile that would have stopped anyone, even as it drew him in. "I'm glad," she said, extending a hand.

He took it hesitantly.

"One less burden."

"I see." He didn't see at all. "Have we met?"

"Call me Miranda."

"It's my mother!" Emily broke in. "Isn't it wonderful?"

Somewhere in the back of his brain, the word "impossible" was jangling like an alarm bell. "But I thought . . ."

Miranda Byrdsong had a very musical laugh. "Oh, I see. You don't know, do you? Of course you don't."

"I heard you were arrested."

"That's true," she said slowly.

"Did you escape?"

"Not in the way you mean."

"Tell him, Mother! Daniel, you're not going to believe this."

"He may not want to hear it."

"No, I do," said Daniel. "Hear about what?"

"Can't you tell by the way I'm dressed?" She twirled once around.

"You look . . . beautiful." He blushed. As a fourteen-year-old, he had no experience complimenting a woman's looks.

Miranda smiled at Emily. "You're right about him," she said. "He's kind."

She turned. "We did our best. There's only so much you can do with a winding sheet."

"A what?"

"I was buried in this."

Daniel blanched.

"I told you he wouldn't want to hear it."

"Are you, I mean, *dead*?"

"I used to think I knew what that word meant. I don't anymore."

"Oh." He felt shy to be talking to a dead person, even such a lively one as Miranda Byrdsong.

"Mother's been explaining things to me," Emily said. "It was awful, what happened. But—here she is!" The girl was so happy to be with her mother again, after hope had long been lost, that she was hardly able to sit still.

Daniel closed his eyes to think, but opened them

no wiser. "I don't understand," he said to Emily. "Where are we?"

"I don't know!" she said happily.

Miranda spoke up. "It's a place called Here."

"Here," he said. "How big is Here?"

"As big as you can imagine, and no bigger. The farmers of Everwood, I have to say, see it as a very small place."

"Because they see it from outside?"

"Exactly. They see it from There."

Daniel, too, had thought the island a small place, until he'd stepped onto it. Now it seemed like a continent.

He looked from mother to daughter, only then realizing that Emily was wearing a pearl necklace. *The* pearl necklace.

"You found it!" he said.

"Mother found it."

"Yes," said Miranda, sitting down and crossing her legs. "The heron brought it to me. Why don't you have a seat?" She indicated a straight-backed mahogany chair that stood nearby.

"Could I ask," he said hesitantly, sitting down, "how you got here?"

"I remember only a part of it," she said. "Mostly, I remember the wall. They took me out and stood me against it."

"The soldiers?"

Miranda lowered her head, remembering. "It was very quiet at first. I had a few seconds to look around. I'll tell you, you pay attention at a time like that."

Daniel nodded.

"I thought they were going to blindfold me, but they didn't. The ground was pretty bare, not much growing, just a little scrub grass and the most beautiful dandelion." She smiled faintly. "Bright yellow! I decided to look at that, rather than at the men with the guns." She paused. "It's strange, but I felt I understood that flower, and it understood me. I felt completely happy. Some of the men, though, I don't think they were happy. Several, in fact, had the good manners to miss. I wonder if they got in trouble for that."

Emily took her mother's hand in both of hers.

"One of them didn't miss. He was a very good shot." Miranda paused. "Very good."

Emily closed her eyes.

"Things got pretty confusing after that," her mother continued. "For a long time everything was dark. Then something changed and I had the odd sensation of being lifted. I remember looking down on the city from a great height. I was being carried through the air, by something warm and strong and . . . bony." She smiled in happy bewilderment. "I woke up here."

The two youngsters were quiet.

Emily looked up. "Is Grandma here, too?"

"Who do you think helped me make this dress? If it weren't for her, I'd be afraid to show myself."

"Can I see her?"

"Of course. Oh, wait. I think she went outside. Said something about taking a walk."

"A walk?" said Daniel. Bridey Byrdsong, at her age and with her arthritis, was hardly one to step out for a stroll.

"Let's go find her." Miranda glided over to the nearest wall. She blew on it softly. As if clearing mist, her warm breath dissipated an uneven section of blueness, allowing her to step through into the sharp greens and browns of a very real forest.

Emily was right behind her, and Daniel stumbled after. He looked around wonderingly at the hazy light brightening the tops of trees. The first birds were gossiping in the underbrush, chirring and whistling and calling out, *per-chik-o-ree, per-chik-o-ree,* while in the distance a faint *peter-peter-peter-peter* echoed through the forest canopy.

If this was not morning, it was an excellent imitation.

Some yards farther on, they came to a large ceiba tree, its thick, leafy branches spread wide.

Miranda was looking up. "Mother!" she said. "Really!"

Emily and Daniel followed her eyes. The first thing they saw were two dangling feet in sensible, square-heeled shoes. Above that, almost lost in the leaves, was a smiling Bridey Byrdsong, waving.

"Hello, children! Wonderful day for a tree climb, don't you think?"

The View from Here

Nineteen

"Mother, what are you *doing* up there?"

"What does it look like I'm doing?"

"It looks like you're trying to break your neck."

For some reason, this struck Bridey as funny. The tree limb shook.

"Hey, Grandma!" Emily yelled up at her.

"Look at you! Come and join me."

Emily needed no encouragement. Grabbing a low limb, she walked two steps up the trunk till she could throw a leg over a branch and hoist herself into the tree. From there, she scampered, branch by branch, to her grandmother's perch.

Daniel shaded his eyes to see. "Mrs. Byrdsong? This is Daniel."

"Well, hello! You coming up, too?"

"I'm wondering, how did you manage to get up there?"

"Climbed, of course."

"But . . ."

"You mustn't think of how I was before. Out there is There. It's how we are in Here that counts."

"Does that mean . . . ?"

"Oh, I'm not *dead*, Daniel, if that's what you're thinking." She swung her legs back and forth. "Miranda's the only one with that distinction. Although," she added, smiling down at her daughter, "you have to admit she's not acting the part."

Daniel glanced at the slender woman beside him.

"Daniel," Emily called down, "you've got to see this view!"

He grabbed a branch. "I'm coming."

Miranda's hands were on her hips. "Well, you can't expect me to stay here by myself!" And she, too, began to climb. She had to twitch her winding sheet free of a twig or two, but she managed to reach a branch not far below the others.

Three Byrdsongs and one Crowley sat high in the ceiba tree, swinging their legs like little kids. Daniel took in the landscape before him.

This was not possible. He'd expected to see the Byrdsong house on its hill, and the road to town, but he saw nothing of the life he'd known. From Here, the view stretched to distant mountains and a waterfall leaping into a misty gorge, while overhead an eagle wheeled and cried.

"We don't have eagles!" he objected.

"Looks different from Here, doesn't it?" said Bridey.

"It's huge!"

"It's everything you can imagine."

"Are there other people here?" he said. "I thought I saw someone."

"What sort of someone?" said Bridey.

"A man. Really old. He was dressed in an old red vest."

"That must have been Jakob. He's my—let's see—great-granduncle?"

Daniel looked confused. "He lives here?"

"Didn't my daughter explain anything?"

"The boy seemed confused enough," said Miranda, "without my adding to it."

"Not confusing at all," said Bridey. "Out there is There." She gestured vaguely. "In here is Here. And then there's the Hereafter. We happen to be Here."

"And you say that's not confusing?" Miranda was smiling.

"I'm just saying, dear, that this is not the final destination. Daniel, you understand me, don't you?"

"I'm trying."

"Don't try so hard. Just look around. How do you feel?"

The boy thought a moment. "Lighter."

"Yes?"

"Peaceful."

"Good. Yes."

The island did feel like a sanctuary, a place where anything was possible. "But you said it's not . . ."

"The final destination? Apparently not."

"You mean you don't know?"

"There are lots of things I don't know."

"But why are we here?" he pursued.

She gave him a motherly pat.

"Grandma says it's because of me," said Emily. "It's a Byrdsong thing. She says we're the protectors of the island."

"*You?*" He didn't want to laugh, but the idea of Emily protecting anything . . .

"Hey, it's not my idea, but it looks like I'm next in line."

"Now that I'm not out There anymore," Miranda put in.

"I see," said Daniel.

"Probably you don't," said Bridey, climbing to a lower branch to be nearer the others. "You see, Miranda was supposed to take over from me, when the time came. But she put it off."

"*Politics,*" said Miranda. "You can say the dirty word."

"Well, you had to follow your own way. I thought you'd get it out of your system."

"It's hard," said Miranda, "to see people suffering and not want to do something."

"You were being a protector, in your way."

Daniel looked from the old woman to her daughter, and from Miranda to Emily. The direct line, with a tragic detour. But it was so pleasant in Here, with the cool breeze in his hair and the leaves swarming about, that it was hard to think of anything as all that terrible.

He thought suddenly of his brother. "Wes will never find us."

Miranda gave him a sidelong look. "You don't think so?"

"How could he?"

"Oh, I don't know." She seemed to be trying not to smile. "What's that over there?" She nodded toward a patch of dark undergrowth twenty yards to the west.

Daniel tried to see. Down among the shadows, he could just make out two faint blue flames. They appeared to be moving.

As they came closer, he saw they weren't flames at all. They were the pale blue eyes of an enormous cat.

Seconds later, the beast broke into the clearing. It was a leopard, creamy white, its long tail twitching. Sitting on its back like a little king, and waving a red bandanna, was Wes Crowley, grinning.

Reunion

Twenty

"Wes! Hey, Wes!"

Daniel practically jumped out of the tree at the sight of his brother. But then he held back. The leopard had stopped short and was eyeing him, its eyes unreadable. It made a low sound in its throat.

"Don't worry about Snowball." Wesley hopped off the leopard's back. "She won't hurt you."

"Snowball?"

"That's what I call her. Hey, Emily!"

"Hey."

He was squinting into the tree. "That you, Mrs. Byrdsong?"

"Good morning, Wesley."

Slowly the whole group climbed down, and Miranda shook Wesley's hand gravely and introduced herself. He'd had no experience talking to such a remarkable-looking person and felt suddenly shy. It didn't help when she broke into a smile, because that made her even more brilliant than before, her high cheekbones flushed with pleasure and her almond eyes shining. It was only when she'd led everyone inside the blue room for a treat of breadfruit pudding and blueberries—a combination as odd as it was delicious—that Wesley began to relax.

"Wow," he said, looking around. "This is some place."

"As long as you like blue," Miranda said.

"Uncle Jakob built it," said Bridey, with noticeable pride.

"It's like we're under water. Like a submarine or something."

Over their second helping of breadfruit, the kids exchanged news about their adventures and the ways they'd arrived at this place.

"You should've seen Snowball!" said Wesley. "She jumped right through this big hoop, just like the circus! I *think* it was a hoop. I couldn't see much, but there was this sticky stuff, and—"

"That happened to me, too!" Emily exclaimed. "Did you end up getting all wet?"

"Ugh, yes!"

"How did *you* get here, Mrs. Byrdsong?" Daniel asked Bridey.

"Uncle Jakob fetched me—very kind."

"Your uncle," said Daniel tentatively, "does he live here all the time? Why hasn't he gone on to his, you know, final destination?"

Bridey nodded. "I'm sure he will one day. But he's a Byrdsong. He still considers it his job to protect the island. Also," she said, "he likes to keep tabs on his house. My house now, of course. One day, Emily's."

"Mine? Really, Grandma?" said Emily.

"Yes, and I hope you live in it a long time. You've got a big life to live out There."

The girl frowned. "But I don't want to live out There. I want to stay Here!"

"My dear," said Bridey, "we need to live our lives—all of us with bodies with breath in them. You'll see."

"I don't *want* to see! I want to stay here with Mama."

Miranda folded her daughter against her. "Of course you do."

"Well," said Bridey consolingly, "we're all Here now, which is a great gift. We should make the most of it."

"Oh, I know," said the girl. "I don't want to waste a single minute."

Wesley laughed. "Hey, Danny! You want to go exploring?"

In fact, Daniel had wanted to explore this unreachable island all his life. "Emily, you coming?"

"Maybe." She seemed torn, wanting to go, but unwilling to let her mother out of her sight.

"You go on, dear," said Miranda. "I'll be right here."

"Promise?"

"You can ride Snowball if you want," said Wesley.

That clinched it. Soon he had Emily up on the animal's smooth back and they set off, the boys walking alongside like her attendants.

H Hide-and-Seek

Twenty-one

Daniel noticed Emily's secret half-smile and thought he understood. Against all probability, this orphan girl had found her mother, and now here she was riding through a mysterious forest on the back of an albino leopard! In what world could that happen?

In this world, apparently. A world called Here.

They went on, following the trails left by animals on their daily or nightly rounds. The vegetation had a primordial look, many of the trees huge and gnarled with age. The lesser trees were equally odd: ginkgos with leaves like little Chinese fans, and monkey puzzle trees, reptilian in their contortions, with spear-sharp leaves growing straight out of the trunk.

Just then a bright-winged magpie flashed down from a eucalyptus tree and landed on Emily's shoulder. It turned and spoke: "*Pjur, weer, weer,*" then flapped to the head of the leopard, right between its rounded ears, and started pecking for lice.

"Cats and birds," said Emily with a puzzled look. "They're not supposed to get along."

"And leopards," said Wesley, "aren't supposed to be tame."

Daniel smiled. "Well," he said, "if Grandma Byrdsong can climb a tree . . ."

Emily was smiling that secret smile again.

"What?" said Daniel.

"I love this place."

He looked up at her, perched on her royal-looking animal. "Do you think she really meant it? That anything is possible here?"

"I don't think Grandma was talking about silly things. More like your heart's desire."

"What's *your* heart's desire, Em?"

"Oh, I already got that."

"Seeing your mom?"

She nodded. "If my dad were here, I'd really have everything. What about you?"

"I haven't thought about it."

"I know what *I'd* want," Wesley piped up. "I'd like to make the clouds come down out of the sky!"

"What!" She laughed. "Why would you want to do that?"

"I don't know. Just to be able to."

Daniel threw him a smiling glance. "Go ahead," he said. "Give it a try."

"Okay." Wesley stood still and concentrated. "Clouds? You hear me? Get down here!"

He looked around. Except for a squirrel jumping between branches, things looked pretty much the same. "It's not working. Of course it's not."

"Hold on," said Daniel as a shadow swept over the woods.

Wesley barely had time to register what was happening before massive cumulus clouds, hundreds of feet high, drifted low over the trees. A moment later, the children couldn't see where they were going.

Wesley jumped invisibly up and down. "I did it! I did it!"

"Wes, you're amazing!" cried Emily. "Wherever you are."

Daniel's reaction was less exuberant. Something about being enfolded in face-tingling clouds made him feel quiet, more inclined to whisper than shout.

Even Wesley's voice sounded muted as he called out for a game of hide-and-seek.

From somewhere, Emily answered, "Wesley's *It*."

"You with us, Danny?" Wesley called.

"I don't mind."

"Okay. I'm counting to twenty. Ready? One! Two! Three! . . ."

Wes went on counting while the other two drifted into the general nothingness. Crouched behind a shagbark hickory, Daniel had an odd sensation—a double sensation, really—a feeling of isolation, as if he were completely alone, and at the same time a sense of multitudes on all sides. Daniel imagined he could see their flittering shadows in the milky light.

"Here I come, ready or not!"

Daniel crouched lower. To his relief, the disturbing shadows had disappeared. Only his brother was out there, stumbling through the underbrush, and Emily, who just then let a giggle escape her.

"I'm coming to get you," warned Wesley in his version of a scary voice.

Daniel ducked lower as the ghost of his brother sneaked past.

"I'm coming to get youuuuu."

The cloud giggled again.

Daniel realized he had not heard simple happiness from Emily before. At rare times, she'd smiled; at others, she had laughed at him, but never *giggled*.

And what about himself, serious, ever-truthful Daniel the Good? He wondered suddenly: *Is it possible, in this place of all possibility, that I could tell a lie?*

The thought was tremendous. Just a simple fib, the kind of thing people tell without thinking.

Sitting in the mist, he tried to formulate an untruth.

My mother is a fish.

He shook his head. *That's not a lie, that's just stupid.*

Far off, he heard his brother's dwindling voice: "I'm coming to get youuuu."

Captain Sloper would never hurt anyone.

There! He did it! No speeded-up heartbeat, no perspiration, no shortness of breath, no headache, nothing!

Mr. Fish is not hiding any chickens.

Easy as pie.

I really hate Bridey. I don't like Dad. I don't love Emily.

Suddenly he really did have trouble breathing. *What* was that last lie?

A deep-throated growl came from invisible underbrush.

"Snowball!" came Wesley's distant voice. "Where are you, girl?"

Another growl. An I'm-over-here growl.

"There you are!"

"No fair!" cried Emily. "Your silly leopard gave me away."

"Now to find Danny."

The voices were getting close. Silently Daniel eased out of his hiding place, and moved farther into the ghostly trees. If he looked down, he could see the ground well enough; but two feet up, things were a blur.

"I hear him over there!" cried Wesley.

Daniel began to hurry, which meant making more noise.

"Go find him, Snowball!"

Daniel broke into a run.

"This way, Em! We've got him now!"

Turning his head to glance behind him, Daniel ran full speed into something—into *someone!*—and they both were knocked to the ground.

When he'd stopped rolling, Daniel looked around, rubbing his shoulder. To his shock, he saw an old man lying beside him, moaning.

"Oh no! Are you all right?"

The old fellow, wrinkled and bearded, winced, his eyes still closed. A fresh bruise glowed on his waxy forehead.

"Mister, talk to me. Are you okay?"

Suddenly Snowball loped into view and jumped on Daniel, knocking him over again. She was followed by Emily and an out-of-breath Wesley.

The leopard turned, padded over to the old man, and, with a sloppy, sandpapery tongue, began licking his face.

"Arrgh!" cried the man, lifting an elbow. "Call off the beast!" Struggling to a sit, he met the curious gaze of the children crouching around him.

"Come on, Snowball." Wesley pulled on the animal's fur.

Tentatively the old man touched his forehead. His bow tie was askew and his red waistcoat covered with dust and leaves.

Emily edged closer. "Are you Uncle Jakob?"

He peered at her through low cloud wisps. "You must be Emily."

She nodded.

"Funny weather we're having," he said.

"It is."

"*I* did that," Wesley declared.

"Did you now. Impressive. Are you all so talented? What about you?" He nodded at Daniel. "What do you do, besides knock over old men?"

"I tell lies."

"Lies. Really. Emily, you have unusual companions."

"I think so."

"They can be our witnesses, along with our animal friend here. But first, I wonder if the young gentleman might do us the favor of lifting these clouds."

"Me?" said Wesley.

"Yes. It would be beneficial to see what we're doing."

"Oh, I can see perfectly well as it is," said Daniel.

"You *can?*" said the little man.

"That was a lie. See how easy it was?"

Jakob looked at him oddly. "Remarkable," he said. He turned to Wesley. "If you please?"

Wesley shifted his feet nervously, not at all sure he could perform the cloud trick backward. "I'll try."

"Try? Here on the island we don't *try* to do things."

"We don't?"

"We *do* them."

"Okay." Wesley frowned hard, gathering his powers. "Cloud? Listen! Here's the thing. Go back up in the sky!"

Everyone looked up into the woolly grayness.

Slowly the bushes and tree trunks became visible, then the middle branches, and finally the swaying treetops. The clouds were on their way into what was becoming a blue sky.

Wesley laughed out loud, completely amazed.

"Thank you," said Jakob. He stood up. To everyone's surprise, he was no taller than Wesley, maybe a touch shorter. Next to them, Daniel appeared outlandish.

"Did you say something before about witnesses?" said Emily.

"Oh yes, quite." The little man straightened his bow tie. "It has to do with your new duties."

Emily looked around at Daniel for help.

"I saw you had the pearls," said Jakob. "I thought that meant you knew why you were here."

She looked down at the necklace. "I came here to see my mother."

"Of course you did. But that wouldn't be enough to get you here."

"It wouldn't?"

"You were allowed to disable the protections and cross over. That's a privilege given to few. The real reason . . ." He glanced at the boys. "I suppose they can hear this, since they've come this far."

"Anything you tell Emily," declared Wesley, "you're going to tell us." His tone was a little grand, but then he was coming off his success with the clouds.

Jakob looked amused. "I see the way it is. Well, then. The

real reason you're here, dear Emily, is to prepare you for later, when you return home."

"But I'm not going home."

He stroked his beard. "A wonderful place, the island; yes, I know."

"I don't care about the island. I want to stay with my mother."

He nodded. "I can see the Byrdsong in you. Strong will. You'll need it out There." He held up a hand to keep her from interrupting. "Come now. No more questions. We need to get on our way."

The Spring
Twenty-two

Emily was not entirely sure about this long-lost relative of hers. "Where are you taking us?"

"To the spring, of course! Climb aboard your leopard."

"What for?"

She felt Wesley nudge her. "Em," he murmured, "don't argue with a dead guy."

"Why shouldn't I?"

"It makes me nervous."

She gave him a look.

"You don't know." He lowered his voice even further. "He might haunt us or something."

Emily turned to Jakob Byrdsong. "You're not planning to haunt us, are you?"

He looked too surprised to laugh. "What an idea!"

"See?"

"I might *hound* you a bit," he said, "to get you to go along with me. What do you say?"

She looked at Daniel, who shrugged and nodded. With a

sigh, she climbed on the leopard's back, and they started off. Uncle Jakob took the lead, stumping along sturdily with his walking stick, while the boys strode alongside Emily and her animal. Daniel noticed the sharp square impression his stick made in the soft leaf mold underfoot. He shot a glance at his brother, but Wesley hadn't noticed.

The land rose up on either side as they entered a thickly wooded valley. Shadows outflanked sunlight here, and the air was cooler. A magpie, perhaps the same one as before, flapped down onto Snowball's head.

Daniel grew thoughtful.

"What is it?" said Emily.

"I'm thinking about Mom and Dad. They've got to be worried."

Wesley looked over. "I told Mom we might be in the woods for a day or two, until the captain simmers down."

"And if he doesn't simmer down?" said Daniel.

Emily looked at them. "Let's not talk about him, if you don't mind."

"We can't just ignore what's going on," said Daniel.

"Why not?"

"Because they're my family. And they're my neighbors. I grew up there, and now Sloper . . ."

"I really don't want to think about it."

Daniel didn't want to think about it, either. He just couldn't help it.

The valley deepened, and the leopard led them down to a boggy depression where giant ferns towered overhead. Emily ducked her head to avoid the fronds. The magpie flew off, crying harshly: *"Wock, wock-a-wock, pjur!"*

A little farther on, they came to a moss-encircled pool with water so clear you could see right down to the rocks, which appeared studded with mussels and oysters. Shadows of small fish darted about in the shallows. *Strange*, Daniel thought, *a spring-fed pool in the middle of an island*.

The leopard bent its head and drank gustily.

"Here we are, children," said Jakob.

It was indeed a beautiful glade, with violets and moss of deepest green, the sunlight complicated by a thousand trembling shadows.

"What is this place?" said Daniel wonderingly.

"The center. It's why we call the island Here."

Wesley squatted at the edge. He cupped his hands and dipped them in. The water was icy.

Jakob stopped him with a look. "I'm afraid it's only for Emily."

"But I'm thirsty!"

"Here," said Daniel, taking out his canteen. "We've still got some water."

Wesley's lips compressed. After his brief time of power over clouds and who knows what else, he was back to being treated like a kid.

"He's probably got a reason," Daniel said.

"I do." Old Jakob leaned his stick against a tree. A wicker basket hung from a low bough; he reached in and took out a silver dipper.

"What's the idea?" Emily said.

"Our family has always tried to protect the island. Your mother can't do it, because she's Here. Are you willing to take it on?"

Emily looked pained. "How can I? I'm just a kid."

"Your grandmother will help you. A drink of this water will help you."

She looked at him doubtfully. "What's it going to do to me?"

"Nothing bad."

"Will I grow ten feet tall, like Alice in Wonderland?"

He shook his head with a smile. "There's nothing magic about it. It just makes things clearer."

"You mean I'll know everything? Like a genius?"

Again the head shake. "It doesn't make you smarter. It just dissolves the barriers. It helps you know what you already know."

"You're talking in riddles." She looked at the brothers. "What do you think?"

"Well," said Daniel, "do you trust him?"

"I guess so."

"You'd better know so."

She looked at the kindly, infinitely wrinkled, wildly bearded face of her great-great-and-even-greater-granduncle.

"Yes," she said.

"Then," said Daniel, "go ahead."

She took the dipper, scooped up some water, held it to her lips, and hesitated. "If I turn into a monster, will you still like me?"

"Better than ever," he said.

"Me too," Wesley added.

She sipped. Nothing happened. She looked around. "What?" she said.

"What were you expecting?" said Jakob.

"Something. A puff of smoke maybe." She took another drink, deeper this time. "That *is* good!"

The boys watched her. "How do you feel?" said Daniel.

"I still don't want to go back, if that's what you mean." She looked around. "Hey," she said, "I can't understand you if you're all talking at once."

"I didn't say anything," said Wesley.

"What do I care if you ride Snowball?"

"I didn't say that." He flushed.

"I heard you mumble about getting to ride Snowball."

"I only thought it."

She turned to Daniel. "As for you . . ."

That was when they heard the first distant boom, more a thud than a boom, like a bass drum wrapped in cotton.

Then a second one. A third. They all looked up.

"The tank!" said Daniel.

There was a screaming across the sky and then a sudden shattering of branches as the first shell hit. Leaves and splintery twigs showered to the ground.

Emily looked around in panic. "They're shooting at the island!"

Part Three
NOW

The Odds
Twenty-three

Emily jumped to her feet, muttering something that Daniel half heard. She said it again: *"Mama."* Another cannon round punched through the air, ripping branches and exploding into the earth. "We've got to get back to her!"

Daniel nodded. "But which way?"

"Snowball will know," said Wes.

Daniel glanced at Jakob Byrdsong.

"Don't worry about me," said the old man, picking up his walking stick. "I'll meet you there."

Emily held the leopard for Wesley. "She's all yours."

"Really?"

"Be quick."

He jumped on and they started out, Daniel and Emily running alongside. The leopard knew the shortcuts, and within minutes came in sight of the ceiba tree at the entrance to the blue pavilion. Miranda and Bridey were outside, talking earnestly with an old man. It turned out to be none other than Jakob Byrdsong!

It registered with Daniel that it was impossible for Jakob to have beaten them there. But that wasn't the only surprise. At their feet, patient as house dogs, lay two beautiful white leopards.

"You're safe!" Miranda cried, taking Emily into her arms.

Daniel went over to Jakob. "How did you *do* that?"

"Be glad to explain," said the old man. For the first time, there was a slight tremor in his voice. "Under calmer circumstances."

Wesley was looking at the cats. "More leopards!"

Miranda nodded. "They're to bring you home."

Another explosion, closer and louder, made them all turn. This time the shell came whistling right overhead, cracking several branches in the ceiba tree and exploding against a rocky hummock. Everyone scrambled to get away from the falling debris.

"That was a little too close," said Bridey.

"Let's get inside," said Wesley, heading for the pavilion.

Jakob waved him back. "No use. I designed the building for beauty, not defense. It won't keep out a fly."

More shells thudded into the spongy air.

"Why don't we just hide out on the island," said Emily, "until they stop shooting?"

"And let the island be destroyed?" said Jakob, giving her a sharp look and waving his walking stick for emphasis. Emily noticed that the top of it was a carved heron's head. "Remember," he said, "you took the protections off when you came here."

"You mean with the mud . . . ?" said Emily.

"Yes. You blocked the signal with it. That's why the artillery can reach us. Now you need to *unblock* it."

"Can we do that?" she said.

"As soon as you're off the island."

"There are three leopards here," said Daniel. "What about Mrs. Byrdsong?"

"My uncle," said Bridey, "has kindly offered to escort me home. I'll meet you back at the house."

"The house? But Sloper's soldiers are all over the place!"

She smiled and briefly closed her eyes, as if to savor the smile. "Look in Uncle Jakob's book."

"He wrote a book?"

"In the library," said Emily suddenly. "Red binding. Is that right, Grandma?"

"That's right, chickadee. How did you know?"

Emily shrugged. "I just knew."

Another artillery shell, higher than the others, whistled overhead.

Daniel nodded. "Library. Uncle Jakob's book. Right." He noticed Emily looking down at her shoes. "It's time," he said gently.

"*You* go," she said. "You and Wes can unblock the protections. You can find the book, too—the second-to-top shelf."

"What are you saying?"

"I'm not going. It's not that I don't care about what's going on out There," she said, "but what can I do? Am I going to fight an army? Here at least I have my mother."

"Is that what you've decided?" said Daniel.

She looked defensive, but stood her ground. "Yes, it is."

"Oh, my dear, no!" cried Miranda.

"What do you mean, no? Don't you want me to stay?"

Miranda touched the girl's cheek. "Of course. But your life is There."

"What if I don't like There?" The girl was dismayed by her mother's reaction, even as, in a strange way, she had already known what it would be.

Miranda sighed. "We can't choose our destiny. I couldn't choose mine."

Emily was getting upset. "Don't you *want* me?"

For an answer, Miranda put her arms around the girl's shoulders and held her close. "I'm trying," she said softly, "to see beyond what I want."

"Mama," said Emily, her voice sounding strangled. "I can't lose you again."

Her mother had no answer for that.

Her grandmother tried for one. "Emily, think what you'd miss by not going back."

"Do you mean war? Murder?"

"Yes," said Bridey. "But also the chance . . ." She searched for the word.

"The chance," said Miranda, "to do something *unexpected*."

"Something unexpected." To Emily, the words tasted like dirty pennies.

"Quite apart from the usual business of growing up," her mother went on, "and falling in love, and one day having a child of your own. That's what There is for."

Now the tears did come, carried by a current of anger. "It's *not fair*!" Emily tore herself away and ran into the woods, ignoring the screech of an incoming shell.

Daniel went after her. He found where she'd stopped and approached slowly, watching her narrow shoulders shake.

"Leave me alone," she said.

"Listen, I understand. I don't know what I'd do if my parents were Here."

She kept her back turned.

"But they're not. They're in Everwood, and they're in trouble."

She mumbled something.

"What?"

"I said, How do you know that? Wait!" She turned around. "You read *what*?"

"I didn't say anything."

"I thought you said you read something."

"Well, I did. I read Sloper's journal."

"How'd you manage *that*?"

"The other night, when I went back for the map. He thinks we're all traitors, and we're hiding weapons."

"How could he think that?"

"I don't know, but he plans to destroy the town, leave not one stone on top of another. That's what he wrote: 'not one stone on top of another.'"

As if to punctuate his words, another cannon volley boomed in the distance. Apparently, the soldiers were aiming at a different part of the island now.

Emily wasn't crying. She was just matter-of-fact. "He'll do it, too."

"I know. It won't be easy to stop him. We need you, Em."

"I'm no use."

"I'm not either, by myself. It took all three of us to figure out the map. We can't do this without you."

"Daniel," she said, shaking her head.

"Okay, then, I don't *want* to do it without you," he said.

She scanned his face to see if she believed him. She remembered that he'd recently found a way to tell lies.

"You know," he went on, looking away and speaking to a nearby beech tree, "I don't have that many friends. I don't like the idea of you in Here and me out There."

She so much wanted to say just then, *I don't either!* Instead, she shook her head. "You're crazy."

"Can't argue with you there."

"You're crazy as a loony bird."

"That's why you like me."

"Who says I like you?"

Good, he thought. *She's back.* "So you'll help us?"

She studied the ground intently. "I don't know. I want to stay here."

"But?"

"My mom and grandmother are pretty strong about sending me back."

"They want you to live your life."

"Do something 'unexpected.'"

"Right."

There was a long pause. She was still looking down. "It would be good to stop that bastard," she said to her shoes. Then she looked up at Daniel's open, hopeful face. "Do you think we can?"

"Probably not," he said.

"Oh."

"Let's say it would be unexpected. Are those good enough odds for you?"

Now she did smile, just a little.

Petals
Twenty-four

"What I can't figure," said Wesley, who never let anyone off the hook, "is how did you get here?"

Bridey looked to the side, as if her smile were just for herself. "A bit of a secret."

"A secret? Tell!"

"Maybe when we get back."

"How *do* we get back?" said Daniel.

"Nothing to it, is there, Jakob?"

"Nothing at all," said the old man, "but when you get across, you must remember to follow the map exactly—*in reverse*."

Daniel promised.

"Everything depends on it."

"We'll be careful," said Daniel. He climbed on the back of one of the leopards. "Ready?" he called.

His brother climbed up on Snowball, but Emily wasn't with them. She was saying goodbye to her mother. Miranda tried to be strong and put the best face on things, but she was wiping away tears. "Go, dear," she said. "Live the greatest life you can imagine."

"But I'll miss you too much," said the girl miserably. "Where will you be?"

"I'll be right here. Now, do you have everything? You have the pearls, I see." They were around Emily's neck. They looked a little odd against the girl's mud-spattered dress.

Miranda nodded. "I'd keep them on."

"Of course."

"I mean *always* keep them on."

"Okay."

"The pearls were formed here on the island. So no throwing them across the stream." Miranda tried for a smile.

Emily fingered the necklace. "Mama," she said, "will you—sometimes—sing to me?"

"I will."

"Promise?"

Miranda enfolded her daughter in her arms a last time. "I promise," she murmured. "Whenever I'm able."

"You mustn't say that. What if you're not able? What if you forget? We have to set a time."

"Em," Daniel called.

"Coming!"

"Let's think," said Miranda. "How about every full moon? Just to make it easy."

Emily nodded. She felt a weight in her chest, making it hard to breathe.

"Now come," Miranda said. She adjusted the pearls around her daughter's neck, then led her to the others and watched as the girl climbed on the waiting animal. The leopards started right off.

Emily tried not to look back, but couldn't help it. There they were, her mother and grandmother, standing in the sunny clearing, waving. She had a sudden thought. Had her grandmother told the truth when she said she'd be meeting them later? What was to prevent her from lying, just to get Emily to go?

Was she lying? Emily couldn't tell, but she found herself memorizing the receding image as if it were already a photograph, yellowed not by sunlight but by age, in a dusty frame. She vowed never to forget it, to keep the image with her, if need be, for the years and decades to come, throughout a long life.

Then the woods closed around her and she had to look where she was going.

Three large leopards strode side by side through the underbrush, their muscles rippling beneath thick fur. They didn't notice the branches that slapped the shoulders and faces of their riders.

"Hey!" cried Emily as a sapling whipped her cheek.

The beast never slowed. It knew where it was going, even if the humans didn't. The woods grew thicker as they passed through a hemlock grove, and the children had to bend forward and low to avoid scrapes. Emily's face was in the fur of her leopard's neck, and she could smell the strong scent of its coat and feel the heat of its body.

Then the woods opened into white oak and beech and the animals were climbing, their breath laboring as they leapt from boulder to boulder until they reached a ridge. Suddenly a vast view unrolled before them.

In the distance, smoke curled up from smoldering gashes where artillery shells had hit.

"Oh!" Emily gasped at the stomach-dropping gorge on her right. Farther off, a mountain rose up, half-veiled in mist, and behind it, just visible, the green-blue of the sea, like an artist's rendition of eternity.

"Is that an ocean?" cried Wesley. "We're nowhere near the ocean!"

Daniel looked over at him. "We're nowhere near Everwood, either."

The big cats started down an incline, skidding a little on the shale, and soon reentered the woods, scrub pine at first, then taller trees. The mountain vista that had so amazed them closed off decisively, as if by a theater curtain. It was warmer here, and zooming with insects. Another few minutes and they came in sight of the familiar woods of their own neighborhood.

Sweating and slavering, the great leopards stopped and let the children slide off.

"This is it," said Daniel.

Wesley winced. "My legs hurt!"

"Look!" Emily said, pointing. "Is that the stream?"

No wide, sluggish current, no vicious snakes, just the quiet chromatic scales of clear water over bright stones.

"We can just step across," said Wesley. A sadness struck him then, and he knelt beside the leopard and hugged its neck.

Daniel was distracted by something overhead, a vague fluttering. "Is it snowing?"

Several white flakes winked in the sunlight. More flakes followed, and more. "It's not snow!" cried Wesley, looking up. "It's petals!"

It made no sense, but there was no denying the delicate reality. Soon petals were falling more quickly, until there was a veritable storm of whiteness.

It lasted for minutes, leaving the children laughing and shaking petals out of their hair and shoes.

"It's the island!" Wesley cried. "It's saying goodbye to us!"

It almost seemed that way. The odd thing was that it was Wesley, the logical one, the scientist, who came up with that explanation.

"Goodbye, island!" he called out. "Goodbye, wonderful island! Hey, Danny," he said, "can we take Snowball with us?"

Daniel laughed. He picked up his little brother, swung him around in the air, and set him down again.

"I guess that means no," said Wes.

"Yes, it means no." Daniel looked around at Emily. She was not smiling. She was not crying, either. She looked forlorn, despite the festive petals still clinging to her hair.

He went over to her. Hesitated.

He put an arm gently around her shoulder.

The Meeting
Twenty-five

"They're after our children!" Gwen Crowley shook her head in baffled anger. "It's bad enough our neighbors have been disappearing, but now they're hunting our *children*!" Gwen was not a person to raise her voice, so when she spoke forcefully, people listened—especially when they were thinking the same thing.

"Let's go and fight 'em!" came a thin, tremulous voice from the back. It was Miss Binchey, the postmistress, possibly the oldest person in town. It was comical to think of frail Miss Binchey taking her cane to the heads of government soldiers, but no one smiled.

The mayor stood up. A tall, stiff man with a face that could have been carved from a walnut stump, Mayor Fench could be counted on to preach caution. He was a man in love with committees, and especially subcommittees, and as a result nothing got done in Everwood. That was fine with the voters, who had elected him twice. Or it was fine until now. "Before we all go off half-cocked," he said in his low, slow voice, "we need to be sure what we're doing. Do we know, for instance, that the children have actually come to harm?"

Dull as Fench was, he had a point. And the answer was no. No one had seen the boys arrested or hurt. Then again, no one had seen Wayne Eccles arrested, or Bridey Byrdsong. Where were they?

"How do we know," Fench went on, "the children aren't just camping out?"

"Actually," said John Crowley, getting to his feet, "they're *hiding out*. Because the captain's after them."

Arnie Fish cleared his throat loudly. "Why would Sloper care about a bunch of kids," he said, "when he's got a war to fight?"

Crowley lifted his hand for silence. "Just a minute." He went to the door and peered from the storage room into the main part of the store. It was dark and silent, as always this time of night. The only sound was the low hum of the refrigerator unit near the front.

"Sorry," he said, closing the door again. "Thought I heard something."

The interruption seemed to sober everyone. Only a dozen people had shown up for this meeting, and they knew the danger they ran.

Min Fish was sitting on a flour barrel near the front. "What if the captain's telling the truth?"

A young farmer sitting near her looked at her doubtfully.

"I mean it," she said. "He said he's leaving in a couple of days, soon's his reinforcements arrive. Maybe he will."

"He's been saying that for weeks," said Gwen. "Why should we trust him?" She pushed back a twist of hair that had escaped her bun. "Obviously, he doesn't trust us. He's confiscated all the weapons he could find."

"Myself," said her husband, "I'd like to know where Bridey is. And Wayne. They didn't just walk off."

There were murmurs of agreement from some, serious looks from all. Everyone loved Bridey; and Wayne was someone they'd known all their lives.

"Is anybody worried about Danny Crowley?" This from a tall bachelor farmer in a plaid shirt. His name was Paul, and he was standing in the back with his arms folded.

"Of course we're worried about Danny!" said Gwen. "That's what we're talking about!"

"Not what I mean." He looked around at his neighbors. "We know Danny's got a problem. We thought it was funny when he was a little kid. It's not so funny now."

"Are you saying," said Min indignantly, "that Danny would talk about us?"

"I'm saying he might." Paul's eyes were black and sharp. "He might not be able to help it."

"Not Danny." Min had always been fond of the boy. Kindness wasn't something you always found in children.

Crowley scanned the room. "Paul asks a fair question. If it will help put your minds at ease, I'll just say there are things we've never told the boy."

"Really!" said Paul. "Like what?"

"Like the things you're thinking about right now."

The two men traded looks like crossed swords. Finally, the young farmer nodded. "Glad to hear it."

"What's that?" Min was looking toward the door.

They all heard it now, the low shuffle of boots just

outside. Suddenly the storeroom door flew open and soldiers burst in with handguns raised.

A moment later, Captain Sloper appeared. He leaned casually against the door frame. "Evening, everyone. Sorry to break up your meeting like this, but which of you is Arnold Fish?"

Slowly Fish rose to his feet.

"If you don't mind coming with us," said Sloper, stepping into the room.

Min caught her husband's arm. "What do you want with him?"

"The charge is serious, I'm afraid."

"That's ridiculous!"

"Is treason ridiculous, madam?"

"What are you saying? Arnie's the most loyal person you'll ever . . ."

Fish patted his wife's hand. "It's all right, Min. I been kind of expecting this." He straightened up. "Okay, Captain. Might as well get it over with."

Protection

As soon as he stepped across the little brook, he felt it, a heaviness, as if the air were less forgiving here, coarser. A great tiredness weighed his body down and made Daniel realize he hadn't slept in some time. The others felt it as well. Wesley yawned loudly. "Do your feet feel heavy?" he said. "My feet feel *heavy*!"

"We've got to keep going," said Daniel. "The opposite way this time."

"Righty tighty," said Emily with a wan smile.

Nothing looked familiar, but the children at last found one of the rock formations, nearly hidden under an entwining of Virginia creeper and poison ivy. Daniel knelt. There was the mud they'd plastered over the spiral-shaped petroglyph. With a stick, he scraped it out, hard and dry as it was, then wiped the place with his shirttail.

"Two more to go," he said.

"Do we have to?" Wesley was rubbing his eyes.

"It's getting late. Do you want to do this in the middle of the night?"

They trudged on. Eventually they found the other two formations and scraped the mud from them as well.

By then, they were ready to rest, but they forced themselves to circle the island twice more. With each turning, the scenery grew more familiar—depressingly familiar, the stream wider and muddier, the thorns sharper, the Uncertainties more certain.

In late afternoon, during their final turn, they very nearly ran into soldiers. A whole swath of underbrush had been cleared, giving the scene the look of a construction site. A dozen men were busy lashing empty oil drums together and laying wooden slats on top. Not far away stood the oversized military tank, the one Sloper had nicknamed "big pig."

"I guess we're back," whispered Daniel.

"Wait!" whispered Emily. She crouched in the underbrush.

The boys ducked down beside her.

"I know what's going on here."

"You do?" said Wesley, who clearly didn't.

She nodded in the direction of Captain Sloper, standing a little way off, conferring with Lieutenant Bailey. "They're making a bridge to the island. Sloper's thinking it over. They're not working fast enough."

The two brothers stared at her.

"You really know what he's thinking?" said Daniel.

She nodded. "He's itching to cross to the island, after

they've 'softened' the place up." She turned to him. "Softened. Does that mean what I think it means?"

"You're the one reading his mind."

"Yeah, but I'm not sure what I'm reading."

"Can you read *my* mind?" said Wesley.

"I'd rather not," she said, smiling. "Way too noisy in there."

"You think," said Wesley, giving her a narrow look, "Grandma Byrdsong can read thoughts, too?"

"I don't know. Maybe not. I think the spring water just sharpens whatever talents you already have."

Daniel nodded. "She has a talent for reading soap bubbles."

"Yeah," she said. "Weird, isn't it?" Her face suddenly darkened. She was looking over at Sloper.

"What?" said Wesley.

"He's about to . . ."

"Lieutenant!" the captain barked. "Fire when ready!"

With a huge roar that made the tank shudder backward, a shell was sent screaming over the island's treetops.

"No," Wesley moaned.

Then an astonishing thing happened. The shell visibly slowed, as if it had forgotten its purpose. Instead of exploding and taking out whole swaths of forest, there was a *phlumph!* and the shell suddenly bloomed into three white birds, flapping harmlessly in different directions, the military scream transformed into birdsong.

The children had trouble believing their eyes. Apparently, Sloper did, too. He was hopping about, furious, and ordered the tank to fire again.

Again the tank let out a belching roar that sent a shell careering toward the island. Again the missile became confused and slowed. And again, instead of exploding in a fiery ball, it burst in a flurry of feathers that flew off, singing.

The soldiers stood staring. Several backed away. Even the men working on the makeshift bridge stopped what they were doing.

"The protection," Emily breathed. "It's in place again."

"Did *we* do that?" said Wesley.

Daniel nodded. "We must have."

"Neat!"

"The captain doesn't think it's so neat," said Emily quietly, staring at Sloper. "He wants to kill somebody."

The boys looked at her. They weren't used to this new ability of hers.

Just then a scream curled up from a knot of soldiers. They were beside the stream, where they'd been setting up supports for the new bridge.

"*It's Martin!*" cried one, backing away.

"Where?"

"I saw him, too!"

"His head! On that snake!"

Even from a distance, the children could read the horror on the soldiers' faces.

Emily's eyes were large. She had liked that young soldier. He'd winked at her at the dinner table that first night.

"Back to work!" shouted the captain, waving his pistol. "I want that bridge finished today! Do you understand?"

Three of the soldiers were walking away from the stream.

Sloper fired into the air.

The men paused. They seemed uncertain which to fear more, the gun or the snakes.

One of them just shook his head and kept walking.

Sloper aimed his pistol. *"I'm warning you!"*

The man kept going. Others started to follow.

The children watched in amazement as the captain squeezed the trigger. The shot was shockingly loud.

Nobody moved. They were staring at the soldier who lay sprawled in the dirt.

"Who else wants to desert?" Sloper shouted.

Slowly a few men, then a few more, went back to work.

"That lousy family," Emily murmured, her eyes half-closed. "That lousy Byrdsong family's behind this."

Wes and Daniel stared at her. She looked at them as if waking up. "That's what Sloper's thinking."

"Not good," said Daniel.

"I guess he hates me and Grandma more than ever."

"Come on. Let's finish this third circle. Then we can rest."

By early evening, scratched and sweating, the friends threw themselves down by the fire pit at the opening of the little cave. Wesley was delighted to discover, this final time around, that his county map and protractor were where he'd left them, a little worse for weather.

Daniel checked inside the cave and found the blankets and cans of food where he'd stowed them before.

Wesley came staggering in after him, yawning fiercely.

It was hard to be sure how long they'd been on the island—time seemed so unreal there, and their energy so high—but now it felt like they'd gone days without sleep.

"Here," Daniel said, spreading out a blanket for his brother. He made another place for Emily, and one for himself. Soon they were snuggled in and drifting off.

All three dreamed of the island. Wesley dreamed he was riding on Snowball and came to a clearing in which stood a gleaming tri-bar—a simple, magnificent shape that doesn't exist in the outer world. Emily dreamed she was in the blue pavilion, on a two-person swing with her mother, talking of important things she wouldn't remember when she woke up. Daniel dreamed of Emily. They were sitting together on a picnic blanket beside the spring, and Emily had just filled her dipper with water and was drinking. It's not easy to drink and smile at the same time, and a thin line of water escaped to run down her cheek and drip from her chin.

As the droplets fell, they turned into diamonds.

Twenty-seven
All the King's Men

Daniel sat up, fully awake. A vague light fumbled into the cave, bringing news of dawn. *Bridey*, he thought.

He stood and brushed the dust from his pants. *We made it back all right, but did she?*

He looked down at his brother and Emily, at the slight smiles playing at the corners of their mouths, and decided to give them a few more minutes. He reached for a can of brown bread and another of baked beans and went outside to start a fire in the pit.

Not a typical breakfast, but the smells of cooking brought the others out, yawning and stretching. All three were famished.

When they were into their second helpings, Emily looked at Daniel. "Yes," she said, "I'm worried about her, too."

"What? Oh." He was still startled by Emily's new ability. In fact, he *had* been thinking about Bridey just then. "Do you think she made it back?" he said.

"We'd better go up and see."

They cleaned the pot as well as they could with what little

water was left in the canteen; then they scattered the fire and set off toward the Byrdsong manse at the top of the hill.

Crouching at the edge of the woods, they looked out across the yard to the house with its pillars and porch. Two military staff cars, like dozing bulldogs, lay parked in the curved driveway.

"What do we do now?" whispered Wesley.

"We cross. There's only one window on this side. It's not likely anyone will see us."

"Okay," said Emily. "Let's go."

They raced out of the trees and reached the side of the house, then listened hard.

"Let's go around back," said Wesley.

Daniel nodded.

The children slipped in the back door and could hear muffled voices coming from the dining room. They crept into the adjoining pantry among the plates and spice racks. At first, they could hear very little. Daniel recognized the insinuating voice of the captain, but couldn't place the other.

As Emily snugged up to the door, Daniel tried to put out of his mind the fact that she'd snugged up to *him* as well.

Then Sloper raised his voice. "Come on, Stecher, you don't expect me to believe that. What is it with you people? Everybody lies to me, and they think I don't notice."

The other man muttered something.

Daniel felt Emily grab his shoulder. "That's my uncle!"

He remembered the surly man in the misshapen hat who'd brought the girl to Everwood. It seemed a long time ago.

He heard a soft gurgling sound—Sloper's flask of calvados emptying into a glass.

"What can you tell me about a map the girl had?"

"Emily had it? You mean the whole time we were traveling she had it?"

"I suppose she did."

The man called Stecher gave a short laugh, like an out-of-breath dog. "Didn't think she had it in her. Mangy little Emily. Nothing like her mom."

"Yes, well, the girl had it. Then I had it. Now nobody has it."

"You mean it's *gone?*"

"Burnt up."

"That's bad."

"Bad, why?"

"It was a treasure map, right? That's what I always thought, from the way old Byrdsong was so secret about it."

"Wrong, Mr. Stecher. It was a map the rebels made. It showed their hiding places, meeting places, where they've stashed their weapons."

"You think so? I don't think so. The old lady wasn't political like that."

"Well, your sister was. The rebels thought she was some kind of saint. She inspired them. They'd have followed her anywhere."

"She wasn't my sister."

There was a beat of silence before Sloper answered. "Meaning what?"

"My mother died when I was fifteen. That's when the old lady had me come and live with her. I never called Miranda my sister. I wanted nothing to do with that crazy family."

"But they raised you."

He snorted. "They took me in, if that's what you mean.

I had to listen to their talk about magical protections and God knows what. They thought they was real special."

"I'm sure you have a sad story to tell, Mr. Stecher, but right now I'm more interested in traitors. Rooting them out."

"Fine. I'm interested in money. Bringing it in."

"Not from me." Sloper took a noisy gulp of his drink. "I know all I need to know. The Byrdsongs are in with the rebels. High up in the organization. Unless you can tell me where the arsenal is hidden, I can't see that you have anything I want to buy."

"I come in here with valuable information."

Sloper took another swallow and let out a sigh. "You come in here with a bunch of nonsense about the Byrdsong family, who, as far as I can make out, did nothing but treat you well."

"I'm telling you the truth. I can prove it."

"You can prove that they're all a bunch of witches and— *what* was it again?"

"Don't believe me. But I lived in this house for four years. I listened and I saw. I bet you never knew about the windows in the Four Seasons room, did you?"

"The what?"

"And that's only the beginning. In one part of the house you can hear the ocean."

"Mr. Stecher, I think you're quite mad."

"Mad, am I? Come up with me. I'll show you the windows right now."

"You're mad, and you need a bath. Why don't you leave?"

"You didn't think I was so mad when I turned Miranda in to you!"

"You were well paid for that."

"Or before that, her traitor husband."

"All good work. Necessary work."

In the darkness, Daniel felt Emily's fingers digging into his shoulder.

"Well," Stecher was saying, "it's the same now. By my count, you're missing four people, the old lady and three kids. Why do you suppose you can't find them? With all your soldiers?"

"I don't know why we can't find them."

"No, you don't, do you? All the king's soldiers and all the king's men, as they say."

"What are you getting at?"

"I'm saying they got things you don't know about. Inventions that can make things disappear. People, too, maybe."

There was silence.

"They got false doors and blind hallways, tricks you could use against your enemies, if you knew how to work 'em."

Daniel was painfully aware of a cramp in his leg, but was determined not to move. He wasn't breathing much, either.

More silence.

"Very well, Mr. Stecher," said Sloper at last. A chair leg scraped along the bare floor. "Why don't you show me those windows of yours."

Twenty-eight
Starting with a Girl

"He's going to tell our secrets!" Emily's whisper was almost a hiss.

The three children were standing in the empty dining room.

"Maybe the captain won't believe him," Wesley said hopefully.

She shook her head. "You haven't seen the windows. Or the staircase that takes you downstairs by going up. He'll believe him, all right."

"First," said Daniel, "we need to find your grandmother. It sounds like Sloper doesn't know where she is."

"Didn't she say to look in the library?" said Wesley.

Emily laid two fingers over his mouth. "Listen!" The sound of booted feet echoed in the hallway. "Quick!" She led the boys through the living room to the pocket doors at the entrance to the library. They slipped in and slid the doors shut. Daniel, who'd never been there before, couldn't help looking around, looking up mostly, at the floor-to-ceiling bookcases stuffed with dusty volumes. An oversized dictionary lay open on a shawl-covered library table near the back wall.

"I used to play in here when I was little," said Emily. "I'd hide behind that table and make up stories."

"Did you ever come across a book by your uncle Jakob?"

"I wasn't old enough to read."

Daniel was scanning the shelves. "A red binding . . ."

She held up her hand for quiet. "They're coming! Behind the table, quick!"

They all huddled down, out of sight, just as the pocket doors slid open and two soldiers entered.

"I don't want to hear about this," said one man.

"You better hear about it. It's getting worse."

"Is it safe in here?"

In the shadows, Daniel looked over at Emily.

"How long have we been in this hayseed town, anyway?" came a voice.

"Lost track. He's got this idea there's a load of weapons here."

"No wonder he's in trouble. He can't go back, you know."

"Don't talk so loud."

"*Meoww!*"

Behind the table, the children looked at one another questioningly. A moment later, Mallow, Bridey's white cat, was behind the table with them, purring loudly. She must have come in with the soldiers.

"Everybody knows he's a loose cannon," one of the men was saying. "And I don't mean the one he keeps firing off into the trees."

The other soldier shuffled over to the library table and flipped idly through the dictionary. The children stared at the tips of his round-toed boots. "So, what are we supposed to do? Desert?"

The other came over and sat on the table's edge, just in front of where the children crouched. "Some already have. Except for that poor lad he shot."

"That was a horror."

"He's getting crazier. He gets these ideas in his head. Now we have to chase around after an old lady and some kids."

"I know."

"*Mrroww!*"

She's hungry, Emily realized, petting the animal to quiet her.

"Besides which, he thinks everybody's lying to him. Well, how can you tell him the truth? He doesn't want to hear that we're losing."

"You think we're losing?"

"I think we've lost."

The soldier stopped flipping through the dictionary. "Look, Bailey, we're not the first soldiers who've had crazy leaders, and we won't be the last."

"So we stick?"

"Long as we can."

There was a big sigh from one of them. "We better get back. They've started firing again."

The doors rumbled open, then rumbled closed.

Emily peered around the side of the table. Slowly they all stood up, the cat circling their legs.

"Bailey," Daniel murmured. "He's Sloper's aide. And *he's* thinking about deserting?"

"What did he mean, 'He can't go back'?" said Wesley.

Daniel pursed his lips. "Sounds like Sloper's got himself in trouble with the higher-ups."

"Whatever it is," said Emily, "we've got to find Grandma. Let's check that book we're supposed to see."

Daniel was scanning the higher shelves. "Is that it?" He pointed to an oversized volume with red velvet binding. It was well out of reach. He pulled over a chair. Even that didn't get him high enough, so he set the big dictionary on the chair and stood on it.

The chair had one leg shorter than the others and wobbled dangerously. Still, he was able to touch the bottom edge of the book and tease it out with his fingertips.

He almost had it. But it was heavier than he'd expected. Still grabbling for the book, he felt the chair tip to the side, and suddenly book and boy went crashing to the floor.

He moaned, but quietly, listening hard. All he could hear was his heart.

Then came the tromping of feet and the two soldiers barged in, staring. Seconds later, Captain Sloper appeared, with Stecher right behind him.

The sitting room was made for afternoon teas, not muddy-booted soldiers, but that's where the children were taken. Sloper threw himself into the flowered chair beneath the painting of the picnic and flicked ash from his cigarillo. "Let's be quick about this. I can't be bothered with children when I've got a war to run. Dominick! Be a good fellow and take them out and drown 'em."

The large person named Dominick flushed.

"What? Haven't you ever drowned a litter of kittens?"

"No, sir."

"Time you learned. On second thought, leave the older boy. I need *one* person who'll tell me the truth."

"Yes, sir. So I should drown these other two?"

"The young one I don't care about. You can leave him. But the girl, yes." He glanced at Daniel. "Why are you looking at me like that?"

"Like what?"

Sloper cocked his head. "You think I'm cruel."

"Yes," said Daniel. "Emily is no threat to you."

"Yeah!" cried Wesley, who was near tears. "She never hurt you!"

The captain leaned back and took in the children standing before him. His cigarillo wove a foul-smelling wreath around his head. "I don't have time for this. I have to get into town. There's some kind of riot by the grocery store."

"My *dad's* store?" said Daniel. "Are my parents there?"

"I suppose they are. Dominick? If you please. You can take Johnson with you. Come right back, though. And then get into town. I'm going to need you."

Daniel took a step forward, though a soldier held his arm. "Wait. What is it about Emily? Why do you care about her?"

"I don't. She's unfinished business, that's all. The family's a symbol, a rallying point."

Daniel's face was hot. "She's not a symbol, she's a *person*."

"To you she's a person. To the rebels . . ."

"I think you're crazy."

Sloper stood up. He wasn't as tall as Daniel, but he was

dangerous. The cigarillo jittered between clenched teeth. "*Nobody* says that to me."

"No one tells you the truth."

Anger blazed, then dimmed. "And why is that, do you suppose?"

"They hate you and they fear you."

"So you're saying they're all traitors."

"I'm saying they hate you and they fear you."

"And you don't."

Daniel hesitated. "I don't hate you."

Sloper smiled just enough to reveal the gap in his teeth. "That's half an answer."

Emily spoke quietly. "Danny, don't bother."

"She makes a good point," said Sloper. He gave a nod at Dominick.

The man saluted and took Emily by the arm. The young soldier named Johnson took the other arm.

"Don't you hurt her!" Wesley cried.

Sloper leaned forward and smiled in a kindly way. "You must understand, I have no wish to harm your friend here, but she picked the wrong bloodline."

"You can't!" Wesley cried, tear-blinded.

"It's okay, Wes," said Emily. As she turned the corner, she shot a glance at Daniel. Her look was unreadable, but there was goodbye in it.

As she was being led out, a messenger passed them in the hall. "One of the farmers," he said, "is refusing to let our men take his soybeans."

"You bother me with this?"

"Sorry, sir, but he's threatening to burn his field."

"What!"

"That's what he said, sir, just before he set his dogs on us. Said he'd rather nobody had it than us."

"Well, he's saving us the trouble, then. We're burning them all tomorrow."

"Yes, sir."

Sloper paused. "Hold on. Maybe we shouldn't wait. Start the burning today."

"Yes, sir."

"Start it now!"

"Hey, you." Emily spoke to the man ahead of her. "Yes, you, Fatty."

No response. They were heading down the hill single file and the path was slippery with leaves.

"Are you going to shoot me, or just throw me in and let the snakes and quicksand do it for you?"

No answer, but she could see the back of his thick neck growing pink. *He's not thinking any of those things*, she realized. *He's just trying to figure out how to make me shut up.*

She knew it wasn't smart to make the men mad at her, but she couldn't help herself. If she was going to die, she'd die spitting in their faces.

They walked in silence. The sheen of the creek was visible through the trees. Emily felt the bumpy line of pearls beneath the front of her dress. Maybe she could bribe the soldiers. The necklace must be worth something. Pearls from the island pools had to be rare. But she dismissed the idea. They'd just take the pearls and kill her anyway.

They were passing the big cottonwood she'd often admired from the top of the house. Beside it waved an oversized rose of Sharon bush.

Goodbye, beautiful flowers, she thought, pausing.

"Move on!" said the man behind her, giving her a shove. That surprised her. He was young and nice-looking, with blond hair and high cheekbones. You don't expect someone with cheekbones like that to shove you.

They continued in silence, finally reaching the water at a place well downstream from the bridge. By then, Emily didn't have a single trick left. Even reading the men's minds was no help.

Dominick was making a great noise whacking away at the underbrush with a machete, opening a pathway. He swore as a branch swung back and stung his neck.

A few minutes later, he called, and Emily went without protest, stepping carefully along.

"All right, then," said the big man when they came to the water's edge. But he didn't seem to know what to do next.

The other soldier looked indecisive as well, for all his good looks and mean thoughts.

For some reason, this made Emily angry. "What's the matter? Do your job! Shoot me. Push me. Do something!"

The silence persisted. They were staring at the water. Rotted sticks and broken vines made Emily think there were more snakes than there really were.

The younger soldier pulled out his handgun, and then Dominick did, too. "Okay," said the first man, "jump."

"Jump? You mean I have to do it *myself*?"

"Go ahead," said Dominick. The anger had drained from his face, leaving it as pale as a pockmarked moon.

The girl looked from one to the other. "You've never done this before, have you?"

"Sure we have," said the younger one, rolling his shoulders.

The big one just looked at him.

"And a girl, too." Emily shook her head pityingly. "It's not so easy to start with a girl."

"Shut up," said Dominick without conviction.

"Even somebody as annoying as me."

"We have our orders," said the big man.

"How convenient."

"Shut up," he said again, but in a voice so low she almost didn't catch it.

During the next half minute, the silence built up like pressure around a diving bell. For all her bravado, Emily found herself breathing shallowly, her eyes following the snakes as they came by, sometimes singly, sometimes in a slither of three or more. Finally, the young soldier could take it no longer. With sudden force, he grabbed hold of the girl's arm, spun her around, and flung her out into the stream.

Just before she hit the water, Emily happened to catch sight of the horrified look on Dominick's ravaged face.

It was the most beautiful face in the world.

Twenty-nine
Uncle Arthur

The boys were seated on heavy dining-room chairs, their hands tied tightly behind them. Arthur Stecher lounged at the end of the table, pouring himself a generous glassful of the captain's calvados. He didn't seem to care that Sloper might not like him dipping into his stock. In fact, after his second round, he didn't care about much of anything beyond his own grievances. His rant against the Byrdsong family had begun to slur, like a dirt road after rain.

He was talking to the world in general and seemed to enjoy his performance more the wilder it got. The boys, meanwhile, were working to undo the ropes. Their wrists were rubbed raw, but they were getting nowhere. Stecher knew his knots.

There was nothing to do but squirm and listen. Time passed with inexcusable slowness. Stecher paused to drink and think, but soon he remembered more wrongs and started in again.

Emily. Daniel's mental processes were reduced to a single

word. He glanced at his brother and saw a tear working its way down his cheek. Wes had to be thinking the same one-word thought.

Emily, Emily, Emily. Enemy. The enemy is killing Emily. There was no thinking straight while Stecher was sitting there reliving the wrongs he'd suffered. Having used up the Byrdsongs, he moved on to Sloper and how poorly the captain paid for valuable information. "Always was a stingy bastard. You'd think, when I handed him Miranda, he'd of been grateful." Stecher thumped his fist on the table.

"Wes," Daniel whispered.

His brother looked over.

"Any luck?"

Wesley shook his head.

Keeping one eye on Stecher, Daniel edged his chair an inch, then another inch, closer to his brother.

"Whatchoo talking about over there?" Stecher growled, remembering the boys' existence.

Daniel tried for a smile. "My brother says the ropes are hurting him."

"Wall, isn' that too bad." He looked into his glass, surprised to find it empty. The flask was empty, too. "Wait here," he said, grinning his yellow-toothed grin as he struggled to his feet. "Don't you go runnin' off, now."

He didn't notice the sideboard and slammed right into it, overturning a serving tray and spilling sugar over the floor. Puzzled, he tucked his chin to concentrate, then wavered out the door.

"Okay," said Daniel, inching his chair closer to his brother. Wesley did the same, turning the chair as he went, until they were almost back to back, and each could just reach the other's rope.

"Quick, Danny!" he whispered.

"Easy does it. Let me get a little closer."

"That's a heck of a knot."

"Hold still." Daniel felt for the end of the rope. There it was. Tight as a tick. He began working it up through the knot. As he tried to visualize what he was doing, he became aware of an oddly sour smell. A rough hand grabbed his shoulder, and he let out a yelp.

"Think you're smart, do you?" Arthur Stecher gave the boy's head a hard downward push and started dragging the chair, with Daniel in it, to the other side of the table. "I can't leave for a damn minute!"

The boy's neck hurt from the violent shove. He closed his eyes. Everything was hopeless. Emily was dead. Horribly murdered. The vision of human-headed snakes slid through his mind.

He had to open his eyes to get free of the image. Turning, he noticed a slight movement by the doorway. There was a sudden loud gong, and Stecher staggered forward, leaning against the table to steady himself.

Standing behind him, soaking wet and holding a heavy saucepan, was Emily Byrdsong!

"Em!" Wesley practically screamed.

Daniel stared.

Stecher had a moment of incomprehension; then he roared and started blindly after her. She backed against the sideboard, holding the pot like a shield, as if it were any kind of defense. He lunged. She ducked away in time. It helped that he was dazed and drunk. He came after her again, and she managed to gong him again, but not as hard, and he easily wrested the saucepan from her. Desperate, she grabbed the back edge of the oaken sideboard and pulled with all her strength, tipping it over. Stecher tried to jump away but slipped on the sugar, and drawers filled with silverware, linens, and candles cascaded down on him.

He lay with the wind knocked out of him. She stood above him, amazed at what she'd done.

"Em! You got him!"

"Wait there!" she called, running to the pantry. In a moment, she was back with a bread knife and cut them free.

Wesley hugged her, wet as she was.

"How . . . ?" Daniel began.

"Tell you later," she said. "He's coming around."

Stecher's head was moving back and forth as he tried to push the heavy sideboard from his chest.

They hurried to the hallway, but there Emily lifted a cautionary hand. Through the open front door they could see soldiers.

A crash of silverware behind them made the children jump. Stecher grunted.

"The back door!" Emily cried.

They ran to the kitchen. Her hand was on the doorknob when she saw, coming out of the woods, the two soldiers who'd taken her to the creek.

"What do we do?" she whispered.

"I don't know," said Daniel. "We need to get to town."

"Mom and Dad are there!" Wesley was breathing hard.

Emily took a key off the nail by the door. "Anybody know how to drive?"

Before they could answer, they heard Stecher's footsteps clumping about in the hall. Trapped on all sides!

"The window!" Emily slid it open and climbed partway out. "We have to go up!"

"Up?" whispered Daniel.

"If we can get to my room, we can hide in another season!" She got her feet set on a trellis bushy with ivy.

Wes looked confused, but there was no time to think; the footsteps were too close. Daniel grabbed his brother's arm and pulled him behind the door a moment before Stecher appeared. The big man let out a belch and leaned against the door to steady himself, pressing the boys against the wall.

"Hey!" he yelled, seeing Emily's foot disappearing through the window.

Stecher stumbled across the kitchen and thrust his head outside just as the girl was nearing the second floor. He struggled out and began clambering up the creaking slats. Somewhere behind him, the staff car roared into life. Dominick climbed in with the others, unaware of the drama behind him, and the car rumbled away.

Emily flung herself onto the roof, then glanced down, her breath fluttering in her throat. The worst of it, she remembered later, was Stecher's Cheshire-cat grin coming closer and closer. In some irrelevant part of her brain, she thought, *He needs a shave really badly*. But it was that crooked, yellow-toothed grin that unnerved her. That and her ability to read his mind. *He doesn't want to capture me. He wants to murder me*.

"Well," he fairly crooned, "little Emily!"

His words seemed to waken her, and she took off a shoe and scaled it at his head. As a weapon, it didn't amount to anything, but the surprise of having it bounce off his forehead made Stecher lurch instinctively away.

The old trellis was never meant to sustain a full-grown man pitching backward. It began pulling free of the building.

He glared at the wall as it moved away from him, as if force of will would stop what was happening. Emily stared, fascinated. It was a slow-motion ballet, the way the trellis arched, and arched further, and then, with a loud crack, snapped. And suddenly Uncle Arthur was on his back in the yard, his body festooned with ivy while his hand still gripped a white wooden cross.

Emily ran to the door leading from the widow's walk to the upper corridor of the house. Her idea of hiding in another season wasn't going to work, she realized, not with the trellis broken and the boys stranded downstairs. Out of breath, she darted down the staircase till she came out in the hallway.

She found the boys in the kitchen. Wesley looked scared. "Did you kill him?"

"Don't know. Takes a lot to kill a snake."

Daniel held her shoulders and gave her a serious look. "And you're really okay?"

She was breathing hard, but she nodded.

"No sign of soldiers," he said. "They're all heading to town. Do you still have that key?"

"Right here." She patted her pocket.

"Then let's get out of here."

The three of them hurried out the kitchen door and across the yard. Passing the broken trellis, Emily noticed her shoe in the grass and snatched it up. She reached the car and slid behind the wheel. "Where does the key go?"

Wesley climbed in the passenger side, and his brother jumped in the back, looking over the front seat.

Wesley squinted. "By the steering wheel, I think."

"Right." She put it in. "Now what?"

"Turn it."

Cheh, cheh, cheh, cheh, cheh, cheh.

"Now what?"

"I have no idea."

They both turned to Daniel. "Don't look at me," he said.

She stared at the three pedals at her feet. "What are those for?"

"Um," said Wesley, tapping her shoulder. "I think our friend is coming."

She looked up. Arthur Stecher had just staggered into view. He was leaning against the corner of the house.

"Damn! Which of these do I push?" Her eyes were on her uncle, who had started across the yard.

"Try one of them," said Wesley. His voice was shaky.

She jammed her foot down and turned the key.

Cheh, cheh, cheh, cheh, cheh, cheh, cheh.

"Try another pedal."

"Another pedal. Right."

"Stop looking at him. Concentrate!"

"Right."

Arthur Stecher had picked up a heavy stick. He felt its heft in his hands. He looked up and grinned that grin.

"Em, you gotta stop looking at him!"

She shook her head, trying to think. "Pedal," she said. She tromped on another pedal and turned the key.

Cheh, cheh, cheh, ChurrurChurrur, cheh, cheh.

Emily looked desperately at Wesley.

"You almost got it," he said. "Try again."

A tremendous whack sent spidery cracks across the windshield.

"Holy . . . !" Emily cried.

Stecher hauled back for another blow with the stick.

"The pedal, Em!" cried Daniel from the backseat. "Try it again!"

With a tremendous crash, the windshield broke entirely, sending shards of glass flying.

"Em! Do it!"

Cheh, cheh, ChurrurChurrur-rur BarRUR-Rur-Rur.

"You got it! Now go!" Wes cried.

"Go how?"

"I don't know. Maybe that lever."

Stecher had come around and had hold of the door handle.

"Lever, lever." She grabbed the gear shift and yanked it toward her. The car gave a tremendous lurch backward and banged into the back wall of the garage, scaring into flight an extended family of wasps. One of them found Stecher's cheekbone.

He let out an oath and waved his arms wildly.

The engine quit.

Emily stared through the shattered windshield.

"Start it again!" Daniel yelled. "Push the lever the other way!"

She couldn't think, but she did what he said. Suddenly Bridey's old rattletrap let out a roar and leapt insanely forward, the front headlight catching Stecher's hip and spinning him against the wall of the garage.

The car rocketed across the lawn.

"Slow it down! Slow it down!" Daniel yelled.

"I can't!"

"*The other pedal!*" Wesley screamed.

She found it, swerving just in time to avoid the big sugar maple by the garden fence. She did not avoid the fence, however.

Sputtering and popping, the disastrous vehicle bumped onto the dirt road that led away down the hill.

Revolt

On their way into town, they were dismayed to see a wheat field on fire, flames twisting in a rising breeze. A half-dozen men were pumping water into buckets and racing to the field, but anyone could see it was hopeless.

The children continued on, silent. Several sheep, clearly lost, wandered across the road, and a number of soldiers trudged by on foot. There was no way to hide Bridey's battered car as it sputtered along. Some odd looks were thrown their way, but no one stopped them. The men had other things on their minds.

"Okay," said Daniel, looking at Emily's face in the rearview mirror. "You gotta tell us what happened at the creek."

Emily was concentrating on driving, gripping the wheel as though it might attack her. "Just let me get the hang of this." She tested several levers as well as the brake pedal, trying to get comfortable with them. "Okay," she said, slowing a little. "The creek."

As soon as she hit the water, she said, she'd fought her

way to the surface, terrified about the quicksand, but also about the snakes. There weren't any at first; the big splash had spooked them, but they'd be coming.

"I remembered what my mom did when she was in front of the firing squad. She looked at something beautiful. So I decided to look up. The sky was perfectly blue—not a cloud anywhere."

"And the quicksand didn't get you?" said Wesley.

"I was careful. I didn't put my feet down. I just kept back-floating the whole time. Floating and looking up. It was like a picture, with leafy branches around the edges and vines crossing it."

The boys looked at her wonderingly. Soldiers, quicksand, snakes, and she could still look at the sky.

"But then I did look around, and I began to see them. First one snake, then several more, coming toward me. There was no way I could get away. I thought of you guys, and I thought of Mama—"

She broke off. Daniel reached over from the backseat and rubbed her shoulder.

"But they never reached me. It seemed that the water around my body was getting clearer, and the snakes wouldn't go there. They came right up to me, but then they veered away. I couldn't figure it out. Then I heard this fizzing sound, quiet, but very close. It was coming from *me*, or rather from under my collar, and I realized it was the pearls! And I re-membered how Grandma sometimes used the necklace to clear cloudy water."

"Wow," said Wesley quietly.

"Grandma told me once that the snakes' poison makes

the water acidic, and that's what they're used to. They wanted to avoid the clear water."

"But the men," said Daniel. "Didn't they have guns?"

"They did, but they missed me. That's another thing. They couldn't miss, but they did."

"Sounds like magic," said Wesley.

She shook her head. "More like conscience." She paused a moment, remembering. "I wasn't all that clear what was happening," she said, "but I think one of them was shooting at the snakes!" She looked from Wesley to Daniel to ask if that was possible. "Anyway, I didn't see the snakes so much after that."

"So the soldiers let you go?" Daniel said.

"They watched me. Then the big one, you know, the one with the face, he just walked away. The other one didn't seem to know what to do. After a while, he left, too."

"I've gotta see those pearls!" said Wesley.

"Sure." Emily slowed some more and took one hand off the wheel to reach down for the necklace. Her expression changed. "Oh no!" She pulled out the strand, to find many of the pearls missing and the remaining ones more than half–eaten away, the nacre cracked and brown. "No!" she cried.

She veered to the side of the road and stepped on the brakes till the car stuttered to a stop.

She held the strand as she might a dead child. The boys didn't know what to say.

Wesley cleared his throat. "I've heard," he said, "that acid will eat away at pearls."

"Anyway," said Daniel, "they saved your life."

"They did." She turned and looked at him. "You're right, they saved my life."

Daniel looked thoughtful. "You could have kept going, right? If the snakes weren't bothering you, you could have kept right on going to the island."

"I thought about it."

"Why didn't you?"

"I couldn't leave you two. You're hopeless without me."

Daniel halfway smiled. "We may be hopeless anyway."

Before long, they arrived at the edge of town. The old car, worn out and mortally wounded, managed to reach Doc Blackman's place, then coughed and quit, expiring in a gasp of steam.

As Daniel had feared, a crowd was milling in front of the grocery store. One voice, then another, rose above the general hubbub. They were not happy sounds.

Wesley looked scared. "Think Mom and Dad are in there?"

"We'll see," he said.

The children hurried around to the alleyway behind the buildings.

"Uh-oh," whispered Daniel.

Up ahead, several soldiers were guarding the grocery's back entry. The kids ducked into a shadowy recess behind the schoolhouse.

"What now?" whispered Emily.

Daniel glanced up. "Let's see if we can get inside."

They slipped around the side of the school building till they reached the door used by the janitor. But the door was bolted and the janitor on vacation. Even the windows were locked.

"Stand back." Daniel picked up a fair-sized stone and knocked out a pane of window glass just below the latch. With all the noise from the street, nobody heard. He reached in, lifted the window, and hoisted himself inside. Moments later, he unlocked the door.

It felt eerie standing in the empty classroom, but they didn't linger, heading instead for the staircase to the upper floor. There they pushed open the door to the roof and stepped out on gravel-covered tar paper.

Emily dropped to her hands and knees, and the brothers did as well, crawling to the front of the building. From there they could see the length of the street. Down by Doc Blackman's office there was no one, but in front of Crowley's the crowd was thick.

"No use hanging around!" A soldier was standing on the store's front steps and shouting into a bullhorn. "The store is closed. No food here!" He sounded hoarse from haranguing the crowd, but they weren't listening. It's hard to argue against an empty stomach.

"Just a minute, everyone!" The familiar voice was Sloper's. He climbed to the top step and took the bullhorn from the soldier. "I know it hasn't been easy, these last couple of weeks."

"What is he saying?" one voice shot out.

"He says we been having it easy."

Sloper was unfazed. "I know it's been tough," he went on. "You'd just sold your summer crops, and here we come along and eat what you'd saved for yourselves."

"You got that right!"

"Well, I have good news for you."

"You got food?" an old man called from the back.

Sloper ignored him.

"Maybe we can get closer," Daniel whispered.

Keeping toward the back of the building so as not to be seen from the street, he took a running start and jumped the scary four-foot gap to the roof of Crowley's Grocery, landing in a forward tumble. He looked back. Wesley had a daunted look, but Emily didn't hesitate. In her light summer dress, she flew like a blue butterfly.

Wesley wasn't about to be left behind. Breathing hard, he ran madly and leapt across. *Almost* across. Short by a foot, his top half landed on the roof while his legs slammed against the side of the building. Daniel grabbed hold of his brother and hauled him onto the roof. Slowly, with Emily holding his arm, Wesley got to his feet.

Daniel meanwhile crawled to the front of the building and found himself directly above the captain.

"The news," Sloper was saying, "is that we're leaving tomorrow."

A murmur went through the crowd.

"Yes. You've been generous and patient, and your country will not forget you. After tomorrow you can go back to the life you know. Food will still be scarce for a while, I'm afraid. There's nothing we can do about that. But at least you won't have an army to feed. How does that sound?"

"He's lying," Emily whispered.

"I know," murmured Daniel. "I've read his journal."

"I've read his *mind*."

"So go home now, friends," Sloper went on. "And go with our thanks!"

"*No!*"

People glanced around to see who had spoken. A few looked up. "There!" cried a woman, shielding her eyes.

Daniel was standing at the edge of the roof. The late afternoon sun was just behind his head, making it hard to look at him directly. From the ground, he must have appeared like an avenging angel. "No!" he shouted again. "Don't believe him!"

Captain Sloper twisted his neck around and squinted at the boy above him.

"It's the Crowley kid!" one man called out.

"He's the one been spying on us," said the man's wife. She spat on the ground.

Daniel raised his arms for quiet—making him look even more the avenging angel. "The captain *is* planning to leave tomorrow," he called out, "after he's burned your fields and barns and slaughtered your livestock! We passed one burning field on our way here!"

"Ridiculous!" shouted Sloper through the bullhorn. "Why would we do such a thing?"

The people looked from the captain to the figure atop the building and back again. It was confusing. Many thought the boy had been spying for the captain, but here he was confronting him.

Daniel looked out over the town. "*Why* would he do that?" he yelled. "Because he has this idea we're helping the rebels. He thinks we're supplying them with food, hiding weapons, who knows what?"

"Nonsense!" Sloper barked. "I love this town!" He looked around at his men. "Would someone please help that boy down before he hurts himself?"

Three soldiers set off at a run. Two others, who'd been

guarding the back entrance, were already inside Crowley's racing up the staircase. They soon raced down again, because the grocery store had no door to the roof.

"And if you resist him, the captain will kill you!"

The voice was not Daniel's. From the ground, it was hard to see who was standing beside him in the blaze of haloing light.

It was Emily Byrdsong. "I know," she shouted, "because he tried to kill *me*!"

Min Fish squinted to see. "I thought she couldn't speak."

Sloper looked as if he'd seen an apparition. "Is that Miss Byrdsong up there?" His shout tried to sound kindly. "Come down, dear. It's dangerous up there for a girl."

"You know what's dangerous for a girl?" she shouted right back. "Poisonous snakes and creeks full of quicksand!"

A woman audibly gasped.

"The bullets fired at me were pretty dangerous, too. For a *girl*," she added with a twist.

"Why are you *saying* these things?" said Sloper. He looked to the townspeople for help. "Why is she saying these things?" He tilted his head back. "Come down from there, Emily, right now!"

"I don't think so. I don't want to give you another chance."

Daniel spoke again: "Listen, everybody. This is real. He's planning to destroy Everwood."

"Why should we believe you?" It was old Dave Tainter, who ran the hardware store.

Wesley spoke up now, his voice thin but carrying. "You have to believe my brother! Don't you know anything? *He can't lie!*"

The crowd fell silent.

"He's got a point there," said Adelaide Fench, adjusting her snood.

"Everybody knows that," Wesley went on. "It's got him in trouble often enough."

The children, with their vantage point, were the first to see the rider galloping toward town. It was the farmhand from Wayne Eccles's place, and he was yelling something. He rode headlong down the main street, his horse at the last moment swerving in a half circle as he reined it in. "Fire! They're burning the fields! Wayne's barn is already gone!"

"Let's go!" a young carpenter named Errol called out. "We'll start a bucket brigade!"

"Too late for that, I'm afraid," Sloper countered, his voice booming through the bullhorn.

At his signal, the soldiers around him lifted their rifles and pointed them at the crowd. From doorways and alleyways, other soldiers stepped out into the street, their guns cocked.

The people glanced around, amazed. A young child started crying.

"Sorry you had to learn it this way," Sloper shouted through the bullhorn. "I was hoping you'd go home and find out about my little surprise firsthand. But the children are right. Even as we speak, the fields are burning." He looked around at the horrified faces. "Soon your barns and houses. Oh, don't look surprised! Just think. You'll be famous! An example to traitors around the country. They'll hear the word 'Everwood' and think twice about rising up against their government."

Paul and several other young farmers made a break for it. A few of the soldiers managed to get off a round or two from their rifles, and a wheat farmer, Samuels, was stung with a bullet in the arm before he disappeared between the houses.

No one else dared move.

Suddenly a man's voice sailed out over the crowd: *"Now!"*

And immediately, in all the second-floor windows, men and women appeared, armed with rifles pointed at the soldiers below.

Sloper's men stared in shock.

The voice yelled out again: "Lay down your guns, soldiers! *Right now!*"

"Oh my God," said Daniel. "It's Dad!"

There, unbelievably, atop the hardware store across the street, stood John Crowley, his rifle pointed directly at Captain Sloper's heart.

"By the count of three!" Crowley shouted. *"One!"*

No one breathed.

"Two!"

A soldier dropped his rifle onto the cobbles. Another laid his down and stepped away from it.

"What are you *doing?*" cried Sloper, reaching for his pistol. "Are you afraid of a bunch of farmers?"

More rifles clattered to the ground.

Cheers broke out around the square. "They're doing it!" Emily cried.

"Now move away!" cried Crowley. "Slowly! That's the way."

Only Sloper and the half-dozen soldiers surrounding him still held weapons. They began backing toward the building.

"Stop him!" cried Miss Binchey, shaking a bony fist.

Captain Sloper raised his pistol in the air. "Don't you threaten me, you filthy peasants!" He looked up at the children on the roof. "As for you . . ." He took aim at Daniel; but just as he was squeezing the trigger, a shot rang out, whizzing past Sloper's head. The captain's own shot went wild as he glanced around, catching the glint of John Crowley's rifle on the opposite rooftop.

"Get him!" screamed a woman.

Without thinking, the crowd surged forward with a roar. It was pure adrenaline-fueled instinct. A few rifle shots rang out, but that only enraged people further as they stormed up the steps, overpowering the soldiers in front of the captain. Some townspeople, farther back, threw whatever came to hand, a hammer, a shoe, or in most cases, small stones from the street.

One of the stones struck Sloper on the side of his head, drawing blood. A moment later, still brandishing his pistol, he slipped through the entrance to the grocery store, slamming and locking the door. Fists pounded on the glass. The glass shattered, and then the door came off its hinges. By the time John and Gwen Crowley made their way to the store and went inside, Sloper had disappeared.

Escape

Gwen hugged her boys tightly, then reached out and brought in Emily as well, like a hen gathering her brood.

Her husband, after seeing everyone was all right, ran to the town hall to release Arnie Fish and the other prisoners held in the basement jail. He came back a few minutes later with Fish and Min.

"Some of the men," he said, "have gone looking for the captain. They're afraid he'll get away."

"All he needs is a car," said Gwen.

Crowley nodded. "By now he must be well on his way to the city."

"But he's not." Emily closed her eyes, as if listening. "He knows if he shows up there he'll be arrested. And to show up without his *soldiers* . . ."

Crowley looked at her questioningly.

"So no, he's not going to the city." She paused again. "He's on a horse—couldn't find a car—and he's heading to the one place nobody can reach him."

"You mean . . . ," said Daniel.

"The island, yes."

"How—?" Crowley began.

"Dad," Daniel said, "just believe her. Come on, we'd better hurry."

They came to the end of the street, where Bridey's car stood, black and dented, looking like a squashed waterbug. There was no getting it to start.

"We'll have to take the buckboard," said Gwen, heading for the shed behind the hardware store.

Soon they were on their way, the kids and Mr. and Mrs. Fish in the back holding on to the sideboards while John and Gwen sat up on the driver's bench urging old Nate, the family nag, to greater efforts.

The captain may have said the farms were burning, but for the most part, his plan hadn't been carried out. In many cases, the men sent to do it had taken the opportunity to desert.

There was the burning wheat field the children had passed on the way in, and farther on, Wayne's blazing barn and cornfield. It was shocking to see waves of tasseled stalks crackling amid the roar of high-reaching flames. The town's one pump truck, horse-pulled, stood beside the field spurting water along the fire's edge.

"It's no use, is it?" said Wes.

"Not much," said his father. He snapped the reins.

Once the flames were behind them, the road looked dim, late afternoon edging into evening. Daniel contemplated his father, up on the driver's seat, the sun striking the side of his face. He was sweating, and his blue work shirt was stained.

"Dad," said Daniel, "all those guns. Where'd they come from?"

His father hesitated. "There are a few things we didn't tell you, son."

Daniel felt his face flush with what he feared his father would say.

Then he said it: "We had a good number of weapons stashed away in different parts of town. Still do."

"Dad!" said Wesley.

Daniel was busy rethinking everything he knew about his gentle-mannered father. Here was a new side of him, and he wasn't sure he liked it. "So," he said, "it turns out Sloper was right."

"Yes, he was right. His mistake was he thought the weapons were stored on the island. A good thing he didn't look behind the walls in the schoolhouse, or in the bell tower of the church."

The buckboard passed the Crowley house and continued on.

"So then it was *you*," Daniel said, "you and the others who brought the Uncertainties to Everwood."

His father didn't answer. Daniel found his silence irritating, as if he weren't owning up to a lie.

"The soldiers would never have *come* here, Dad. Sloper would've left us alone. But he knew . . ."

Gwen laid a hand on her son's shoulder. "Sometimes you just have to step up and do something."

Wesley looked at her. "Did you know about this, Mom?"

"Your mother kept track of everything," said Crowley. "What we had, where it was stored, when to send the next shipment to our friends in the city." He glanced back at Emily. "I don't suppose you know where the captain is now?"

"Not exactly. I just know he's desperate to get to the island."

"If you say so," said Crowley. He turned the horse toward the pathway into the woods. "We'll take the wagon as far as we can. Arnie, do you and Min want to get out here?"

"And miss this?" said Min.

Crowley nodded. "Okay, then."

The sky was still blue overhead, but the trees deeply shadowed, as if they knew more about night than the rest of us. The big cottonwood down the hill from Bridey's was darkest of all. A few feet away stood the tall rose of Sharon, its large pink blooms going gray in the failing light. Nearby, continually whispering, ran the insidious stream.

The way through the woods was easier than expected, since the tank had come this way before, flattening the underbrush. Seeing a glint of water ahead, Crowley tethered the horse and climbed down. He slung a canvas tool bag over one shoulder and led the way on foot. Behind them, unnoticed, trotted the cat Mallow, half-visible among the leaves.

Before long, they came to the edge of the torn-up area where the tank stood, huge and useless, steeped in shadow. Gray in the fading light, Mallow darted ahead, then stopped to sniff about. The scene looked different, even from yesterday, when the makeshift bridge had been lying on the ground, the empty oil drums lashed together and covered with planking. Sloper had managed to push the thing, barrel by gonging barrel, into the stream till one end of it touched the island. He was at the water's edge now, bent over his work, making fast the near end while the barrels bobbed gently like a necklace of coal.

Sloper straightened up and saw them. "Hello, traitors," he said.

"Good evening, Captain," said Crowley, stepping closer. "Quite a contraption you've got there."

Sloper glanced at his handiwork. "It'll serve the purpose."

"I'm afraid we can't let you use it." He pulled out a pistol.

"You don't want to do that, John," the captain said. "Put it away and I promise I won't mention it in my report."

"Your what?"

"You do realize it's a crime to threaten a member of the armed forces."

"Please keep your hands out to the side, Captain. . . . Captain? *Now!*"

Sloper sighed and held his hands out. "You're getting in deeper and deeper, John. I won't be able to help you."

"Arnie," said Crowley quietly, "would you mind taking the captain's gun?"

"Wouldn't mind at all!" Mr. Fish approached the captain cautiously, as he might a copperhead. Circling behind Sloper, he reached out slowly and unsnapped the holster. He was gleeful when he returned to the others.

"You be careful with that, Arnold Fish," said Min. "I think you better give it to me for safekeeping."

"It's safe enough with me, old girl," he said, turning the pistol from side to side, admiring it. "Unless I get nervous and accidentally shoot his head off!"

Wesley giggled nervously.

"Danny," said Crowley, keeping his eye and pistol steadily on the captain, "take a look in that bag. See if there's any rope."

Daniel rummaged among the tools and found it.

"Good. Can you cut a piece, maybe four feet?" He watched as his son hacked off a length. "Now, while Arnie and I have the captain covered, I'd like you to go behind him and tie his hands. Can you do that?"

The boy nodded. "Sure."

"I wouldn't," said Emily. "His thoughts are jumping all over the place. I can hardly keep track of them."

"Careful now, son," said Crowley as the boy circled around.

The captain looked amused at all the precautions. "Don't be afraid, my friend," he said as Daniel came up behind him. "I won't bite you."

"I'm not your friend."

"Honest as ever."

Daniel came closer. "Please put your hands behind you."

"Listen," said Sloper, dropping his voice so the others wouldn't hear, "why don't you just come with me to the island? We'll have a grand adventure."

"Your hands, please."

"Come on. You know you've always wanted to go. They won't shoot if you're with me. Then we'll cut the bridge free and they won't be able to follow."

"I've already been there."

"You what!"

"I decided to come back."

"Very well," Sloper sighed. "Live your dull little life." He reached his hands behind him.

Daniel made a slipknot and started to loop it around the captain's wrists.

Sudden chaos! Sloper caught Daniel's wrist and spun him around, holding him tightly in front of him like a shield. At the same time, Daniel felt something metallic and very sharp against his neck.

No one moved. They seemed paralyzed.

"All right," the captain snapped, "listen, everyone. This is how it will be. You'll drop your weapons and leave. Understand?"

"Don't you hurt Danny!" cried Gwen.

Crowley held his wife's arm. He regarded Sloper gravely. "If you harm my son . . ."

"He's my ticket out, that's all."

"And afterward you'll let him go?"

"Trust me."

"*Trust you?*"

"Or don't. But lay down the gun. You too," he said, nodding at Fish.

Crowley lowered his pistol and let it drop to the ground. After hesitation, Fish did the same.

"Now get out of here."

Daniel felt the blade jiggle against his neck as the captain spoke. He tried not to breathe.

He saw his parents back away.

"Looks like we'll be having our adventure after all," Sloper murmured, dragging Daniel backward onto the bridge.

There was no handrail or even guide rope to hold on to,

and the whole structure was bowing in the middle under the pressure of the current.

"Let me go!" cried Daniel. He struggled, but carefully: the blade trembled an inch from his throat.

"I don't think so."

They were several feet out from land, and already the bridge was bouncing underfoot like a trampoline.

"You don't want to do this," Daniel said.

"But I do." He dragged the boy a few feet farther.

"Listen. It's not so easy to get to the island. If it were, people would've built a bridge long ago."

"They're stupid farmers. What do they know?"

When they were halfway across, the bridge dipped under their weight, soaking their shoes and throwing their balance off. They almost went in right then.

"The place is protected!" Daniel cried out.

"What are you gargling about? Come on!"

Daniel had to say it. *"It's where you go after you die!"*

Sloper paused. "You really can't lie, can you? You try and you come out with gibberish."

The bridge swayed and Daniel slipped, landing hard. He lay facedown and held on to the edge of the planking.

"Steady!" Sloper cried. His arms windmilled as he fought to keep himself from falling. It was obvious he couldn't fight Daniel and still make it across. He took a final look back. "Not coming?"

Daniel shook his head.

"Then *damn* you, Daniel Crowley!" Sloper turned and went on alone, his arms waving about as the planks lifted and fell beneath him.

He was most of the way across when a low growl stopped him cold. At the far end, with fangs bared and lips blackly curled, crouched an appalling white leopard.

Sloper let out a cry, almost losing his balance, but managed to turn and start back toward Everwood. That's when the little white cat, Mallow, jumped onto the bridge. It stepped on Daniel's shoulder and walked down his back, its eyes fixed on Sloper. With each step, the creature grew bigger, and finally *huge*—transformed, in fact, into a second leopard as fierce as the first.

The sunset caught a gleam of fear in Sloper's widened eyes as he stepped backward, his arms flailing and the planks beneath him wobbling dangerously from side to side.

The leopard that had been Mallow crept slowly toward him, its head low.

"Get back!" Sloper shouted. He waved the knife blade threateningly, but it had no effect except to make the bridge quiver and roll. All the stresses began to loosen the lashings, and one of the barrels, then a second, broke free of the rope bindings and floated off.

"Ahh!" Sloper cried, struggling frantically to keep his balance. He teetered a final moment, then tumbled backward into the stream.

The splash he made hitting the water nearly upended the bridge, and Daniel, still on his stomach, gritted his teeth and gripped the planks with all his strength.

His situation abruptly worsened. The lashings fell away entirely, and the boards began separating beneath him. He heard voices shouting to him from shore, but all he could think was that he was now half submerged in snake-infested water and sinking fast. Desperate, he reached out and grabbed on to one of the floating barrels. It supported him, precariously, but left his legs hanging in the murk, his feet grazing the quicksand.

A second barrel floated within reach, and he managed to pull it against the first, hoisting himself mostly out of the water. Holding the barrels together took all his concentration.

"Son! Son!"

He was finally able to distinguish his father's voice from the general roaring in his brain.

"Dad!"

"I'm throwing you a rope. Try to grab it!"

Through the twilight air Daniel saw the rope in flight, a brief hieroglyph against the still blue sky, before it splashed into the creek just out of reach.

"Try it again, Dad!"

Mr. Crowley hauled the rope back and again hurled it, this time landing it almost beside the boy. Daniel grabbed it tightly but, in doing so, lost his grip on one of the barrels. The whole lower half of his body sank into the water.

"I've got it! Hurry, Dad!"

His father began pulling, hand over hand.

A plank floated by. Then a snake, its head just above the waterline. Daniel froze. And was that another one, just behind the first?

"Hurry, Dad!"

The barrel, with Daniel clinging to it, continued to move toward the shore. But then his foot, dragging along the muddy streambed, caught on something—a rotted branch or vine, or maybe something worse. His father pulled, but Daniel and his barrel were stuck.

Daniel panicked at the sight of more V-shaped ripples just upstream from him. He twisted his leg around frantically until his shoe came off and he was free.

"Hang on, son!"

"Danny!" It was Emily's voice. "You're almost here!"

He was moving again toward shore. Toward her.

"I'm coming!" There were snakes; there was quicksand; but he just looked at Emily. Emily getting closer.

Very close now.

He felt his father's strong grip on his arm, pulling him up, holding him steady. It was only then that the tears came.

Through blurry eyes, he could see Emily and Wesley. She flung herself against him. "You're all right? You're *really* all right?"

Somebody was shouting. "Down there!"

"Where?" called another voice.

A group of townspeople came up, breathing hard, some with lanterns, several with rifles, even one woman shaking a hay fork. They all watched the water in silence as the remnants of the bridge drifted slowly by.

Daniel made his way to the stream's edge with Emily and Wesley beside him. In the dimming light, the ripples gleamed like oil, reflecting the sky and trees.

"It's a cursed place," muttered the young farmer named Paul.

No one contradicted him. All were noticing the

disturbances in the surface, the slow, V-shaped ripples made by the water snakes.

The men held up their lanterns. Most had never been this close to the stream before, barred by thorns and warned away since childhood by scolding parents. Under the swaying light of the lanterns, they could see the heads clearly. Human heads, each one distinct.

As they watched, one snake, larger than others, slid by close to the shore. Daniel gasped. His father stepped back. In later days, the townspeople would argue about what they'd seen, but it was impossible to mistake the features of Captain John Sloper, his eyes glinting, his mouth curled in a serpentine snarl.

Thirty-two
Jakob's Trick

"There we go."

Daniel hefted the heavy volume and opened it on the table. It was an oversized book titled *The Book of Impossibilities*. Only the initials J.B. indicated an author. There was no publisher; in fact, the whole thing was handwritten, in careful calligraphy, with many drawings and diagrams. The last third of the book, the children discovered, consisted of architectural plans for Bridey's house.

"I don't get it," said Daniel. "How's this book supposed to help us find your grandmother?"

Emily closed her eyes, as if a thought were at the tip of her mind. "I think Grandma meant us to look at the diagrams for this room."

"Why would you think that?" said Wesley.

"Just a feeling."

Daniel had already begun leafing through the volume. He stopped when he came to facing pages about the library and pulled the gas lamp closer. His hand trembled. Not

surprising. It was nine-thirty at night, and he was still shaken by the events of the day. If he closed his eyes, he could see the collapsing bridge and the terror in Sloper's eyes. He tried to concentrate, but the diagrams, arrows, letters, and labels wouldn't stay still.

"What's this?" said Wesley, looking over his brother's shoulder. "It looks like an alcove."

"So?"

"Look around. Do you see an alcove?"

There wasn't any.

"It's supposed to be over there." Wesley pointed to a shadowy corner of the room, where the bookshelves rose nearly to the ceiling.

The children looked carefully, Daniel feeling along the higher shelves, Emily on her knees. They were almost ready to give up when the girl pulled out a big book on ornithology and felt behind it.

"Ha!" she exclaimed as her fingers found a small, trigger-like projection.

She pushed it. Nothing. Pushed it harder. Nothing again.

Finally, it occurred to her to pull it. There was a metallic cluck, followed by a faint groan, as a wall panel, five feet high, swung open on hinges.

Silently they looked in.

Darkness.

Holding a candle before him, Wesley led the way, shadows dancing along the walls and ceiling. The space was narrow and draped with cobwebs. Papers, books, and yellowing scientific journals filled the shelves above a dusty desk. But there was no room to move around because covering the floor in the center of the room was a flowered quilt. Sprawled across it lay a large woman. She wasn't breathing.

"*Grandma!*" cried Emily.

Hesitantly the girl approached. She knelt. Touched the old lady's shoulder. "Grandma?"

No response.

She shook the shoulder.

Nothing.

"Grandma, *wake up!*"

Wesley took hold of Bridey's wrist and felt for a pulse. "I don't feel anything!"

The children fell silent, awed by the lifeless form before them.

Emily tried to read the woman's thoughts, but couldn't sense any. Finally, she flung herself over her grandmother's body. Tears wet the old woman's nightgown. "No, Grandma! Don't be dead!"

Daniel felt close to tears himself. He loved Bridey Byrdsong. He'd loved her all his life. "Anybody know artificial respiration?" He looked around desperately, but the others only shook their heads.

"Breathe!" cried Wesley.

Just then the cat padded in, curious about the commotion. It looked around, then stepped gingerly on the quilt.

Instinctively Daniel backed away, remembering Mallow's transformation on the bridge. There was nothing ferocious about the little animal now. It walked over Emily's back and went up to Bridey's face.

"Go away, Mallow," said Emily.

The cat sniffed Bridey's cheek. It began licking her chin.

"Wait," said Wesley, who was holding the woman's wrist, "I think I feel something!"

Mallow purred and licked.

Bridey's eyes trembled slightly, then fluttered open. "Mallow," she said. "Stop that, you silly thing!"

The stunned children stared.

Bridey squinted back. It seemed to take an effort to focus, and the flickering candle didn't make it easier. "Well!" she said.

"Grandma!" Emily cried. "You scared me to *death*!"

"Did I?" She looked confused.

"I couldn't hear your thoughts and I was afraid . . ."

"Were you? I suppose I was pretty far away."

Emily seemed caught between a smile and a tear. "Oh, Grandma!"

Bridey closed her eyes to remember. "I was on the island with Jakob and Miranda. Wait," she said. "I'm not in my own room, am I?"

Daniel spoke. "You're in an alcove behind the library."

Bridey's eyes widened. "Where's Jakob?"

"He's not here," said Daniel.

"No, of course he's not." She shook her head to clear the confusion. "He never stays."

"How'd you ever get in here?" said Daniel.

She was still putting it together. "Well," she said, "I had

to park my body someplace safe." Wincing, she sat up. "Same old aches and pains, I see, just waiting for me to come back. Hello, aches and pains. Did you miss me?"

Wesley shot a look at his brother. "She's delirious."

"I don't think so." Emily was beginning to smile. "I think it's that same trick Uncle Jakob did with his dog. Right, Grandma?"

"You *are* a smart one."

"What dog?" said Wesley, bewildered.

Emily explained about Jakob's dog, Bounce, and how he had looked dead but wasn't.

"Well," Bridey interrupted, as if stating the obvious, "you don't think this old body could have gotten to the island the way *you* did, crawling around under thorn bushes!"

Bridey struggled to get up then, but couldn't manage it. "Could you dear people help me back to my room? I'd like to freshen up."

"Maybe you should wait a bit, Mrs. Byrdsong," said Daniel.

"Wait?"

"Till you're a little steadier?"

Bridey rubbed her forehead with a knuckle. "I suppose you're right. Oh," she said, suddenly wide awake. "I'd forgotten about that awful Captain Sloper. Do you suppose he's still angry at me?"

"Grandma," said Emily, "I don't think you need to worry about Captain Sloper."

"Really?" She looked at her granddaughter narrowly.

"You've got a sly look, Emily Byrdsong. What have you done with him?"

"Danny did it."

Bridey turned wondering eyes on the boy.

He shook his head. "I didn't do anything."

"You did him in, didn't you?"

He laughed. "Your cat did him in."

"What? Mallow?" She scratched under its chin. The cat purred loudly. "Why, she wouldn't hurt a flea!" She paused. "Or maybe she would. Did she?"

"She scared him into the creek," said Daniel. "Scared me, too."

"Naughty cat." She pulled it onto her lap. "You know about cats. Regal creatures." Color was coming into her cheeks as she spoke, as if the subject put life in her. "Out here they're kitties. But on the island they take their true form."

Wesley was looking from her to the cat and back again.

"I call her Mallow," she said, "after those lovely flowers by the island. But you can just as easily use the name Wesley came up with."

The boy's eyes widened. "Snowball!" He scooped the creature into his arms.

"Snowball, it's you!"

Thirty-three

Something Unexpected

It rained that night, hard enough to suppress the few fires the soldiers had managed to start. Daylight came with sullen clouds and the stink of charred wood. Emily sat on the roof with Mallow in her lap. Across the woods lay the island, as beckoning and unreachable as ever. At least her grandmother was home. It must have been hard for her to return and accept the aches and illnesses that had plagued her so long.

She'd been climbing trees on the island. Climbing trees! Back home, she could barely climb the stairs. Yet she'd chosen to return.

Emily didn't know if she would be so generous.

"Hey, Em, you up there?"

She ran to the edge of the widow's walk. Below, standing in the curved drive, were the Crowley brothers, Daniel with a saw over his shoulder. She waved. "Come on up!"

"Wish we could," Daniel said. "A bunch of us are heading to Eccles's place to help rebuild the barn. Want to come?"

Did she want to help build a barn?

"I'll be right down."

In the days ahead, there was much work to be done, and everyone's help was needed. Sometimes Emily almost forgot about the island.

But one night, just as the full moon approached, she was lying up on the roof with Mallow, staring at the constellations that weren't entirely obscured by moonshine, when she heard a distant voice. She sat up. Then she stood up. It was a woman's voice, singing!

"Mama!" she cried, hurrying to the wrought-iron railing at the roof's edge. "Mama, I hear you!"

The voice went on, song after bedtime song, like a silver ribbon unspooling through the dark. Emily scarcely noticed the cat rubbing against her legs, or the moon-silvered tear working down her cheek.

The next day, she told Daniel her plan. She would go back to the island. He could come with her if he wanted. He could even bring Wes.

"Don't try to talk me out of it. She's right there. She was singing to me. What's to stop us?"

At lunch that day (her grandma's special: egg-salad-and-watercress sandwiches on lightly toasted cheese bread, with the edges cut off), she broke the news. The old woman stopped eating.

"What's the matter?" said the girl.

"I'm afraid it's not possible."

"What do you mean? Of course it's possible! We did it before."

Bridey set her sandwich on the plate. "That doesn't mean you can do it again."

She saw Emily's look.

"Don't be angry, dear," she said. "You'll learn many things as you grow up. You may even learn ways to get back to the island."

"Like the way you went?"

"Ah," said Bridey. "That was a trick Jakob taught me. It took years to learn."

Emily jumped up. "I don't care what you say; I'm going back to be with my mother! You'll see!"

She stormed out and ran down the road and across a field to the Crowleys' house, where she found Daniel stacking firewood out back. She spoke in such a rush that he didn't catch it all.

He rested his hands on his hips. "Well, we did it once. Let me get Wesley."

She wiped her tear-smeared face, aware suddenly that she'd been crying in front of a boy. Of course, Daniel wasn't a boy, not what she thought of when she thought of boys. He was better.

"Here," he said, offering his sleeve.

She looked at him questioningly. Then she bent toward the sleeve and wiped her nose on it.

***

The wind was picking up by the time they reached the cave. Everything was as it had been before—the tools and cooking utensils on the shelf inside, the fire pit out front. Emily was ready with her pail of dirt from next spring.

On all sides, the tops of trees were sighing. The whole forest, it seemed, was excited. Even the clouds ran races.

"Hope it doesn't rain," said Emily.

"Looks like it might," said Wes.

Daniel pursed his lips. "Okay. We're looking for three stone markers, starting with this one."

They poured some water in the pail to make mud, then smeared it over the spiral petroglyph.

"Righty tighty," murmured Emily. "Lefty loosey."

The way around the island was difficult, but they kept on, reaching the other two formations. More mud. Pushing on, they completed three circles, arriving back at the campsite scratched, exhausted, and windblown.

They were no further back in time than when they'd started, and the creek was no narrower.

"It's not working!" cried Emily.

"Let's take a break," Daniel said.

They walked along through the woods till they came to the path that led to the wooden bridge.

Wesley climbed up and straddled the railing. He turned to Emily. "Mind if I look at those freckles again?"

She sighed. "Okay. Sure." She leaned against the rail and let him pull the shirt away from the back of her neck.

"Where are they?"

"Where are what?"

Daniel was looking, too. "They've faded. I can't see anything at all!"

"*What!*"

"Nothing there," said Daniel. "It almost seems like we're not supposed to do this."

"But I've got to see my mom!"

"I know, Em."

"Don't I?" Suddenly she didn't seem sure.

"I don't know." He stared at his shoes, thinking. "She did say, didn't she, that she wanted you to live your life out here."

"Yeah," she said bitterly. "Where I could do something unexpected."

"Well, we've done one thing I *never* expected," he said. "We beat Sloper."

"We did."

Daniel could tell this gave her comfort.

"We did do that. Still . . ." Her voice trailed off.

"Still you miss her," Daniel completed.

That's when Wesley spoke up. "Hey, look what I found in my pocket!" He pulled out a creased and dirty piece of paper. It was the copy he'd made of her freckles.

"Let me see!" Emily took it and spread it open on the railing.

But just as she was starting to examine it, a gust of wind snatched it away.

"Oh!" she cried out.

They watched the map somersault through the air, tumbling high above the creek. It landed finally in a stand of rose mallow flowers on the other side.

Daniel moved close to her and she buried her head against him. "Maybe it's all right," he said quietly, "living here with us."

Maybe it was, but she wasn't ready to hear it.

"Danny, look!" said Wesley. "It's him!"

Stately as a church elder, feathers riffling, the great blue heron paced the other shore. The first fat drops of rain hit the railing of the bridge, but the children didn't notice. They were transfixed by the slow-motion dance before them.

Tilting its head one way, then the other, the creature bent toward the paper as if to see what it was—then suddenly stabbed it with its beak.

For long seconds, the great bird stood immobile. Finally, it turned, the map still impaled, and walked slowly away.

Acknowledgments

Special thanks to my Braintrust, an elite group of readers I turn to when I can't see my way ahead. You always get me back on track. Thanks, also, to my insightful editor, Nancy Siscoe, for her fine eye and blue pencil, and to my artful agent, Jodi Reamer, for guidance and great lunches.